PROLOGUE

*Z**oey Parker's limbs felt heavy as she tried to open her eyes. When they finally cooperated, she jolted upright. She was on a bed she didn't recognize. Her dress was ripped, her breasts exposed. Between her legs, her underwear was gone. She frantically scanned the sheets, searching for signs that her virginity was still intact. She didn't find blood on the bed or between her thighs.*

A rush of heat stormed over her as her stomach flipped and skin crawled. Needing to rid herself of it all, she ran to the trash can in the corner of the room and threw up twice. After she emptied her stomach, she gulped down shallow breaths to stay calm. A quick survey of the room, and she found a sweater lying in a heap. She threw it on and was out the door a second later. The scent of beer hit her nose as she made her way down the staircase. Plastic cups littered the hallway and the stairs. Passed out bodies were every-where, sleeping off the booze from the fraternity party the night before.

She didn't think she'd drank that much. Three drinks, she remembered. The rest...the rest of the night was dark.

When she made it outside, she decided to walk instead of

1

waiting for a Lyft. Each bare-footed step felt like it took a lifetime, and the world seemed so far away.

"Miss. Miss."

Zoey blinked, finding a woman with a kind face pulling up next to her.

"Are you okay, honey?" the woman asked gently.

Her breath became stuck in her throat, the inside of her body wanting to flip itself on the outside just to repel the unwanted feelings. "No," she whispered. "No, I don't think I am."

Zoey shook her head, pulling herself out of the memory. She still felt foggy two days later. Her skin still crawled whenever she thought about what might have happened. She wasn't sure if it was a blessing or a curse that she had no recollection of that night. She didn't feel like she knew anything anymore. Except that New York City no longer felt safe. *She* didn't feel safe.

Laughter and voices carried across the warm breeze while she sat beneath a tree, trying to focus on writing her paper. In only a few months, she'd finish up at New York University and apply for veterinary college. All of her hard work would soon pay off. The long nights of studying, the lack of a social life, were all worth it. She missed her home in Sacramento, California, where her happily married parents lived. Once her schooling was finished, she'd go back home to her family and her high school friends. To get the life she was working so hard for. She tried to focus on that future and forget the pain from two nights ago.

When a shadow passed over her, it stole the warmth of the sun. Zoey glanced up, finding her two friends, Julie and Ava, standing above her. Both were in the same Biological Science course. On the first day of freshman year, they had all clicked. So much so that, eventually, they'd all rented an apartment together. Where Zoey considered herself more natural in style, Julie and Ava always had their makeup and hair done to perfection. She envied that about them as much as their outgoing personalities. But now, they both looked pale, eyes glassy. "What's wrong?" Zoey asked, setting her laptop aside on the grass.

"I'm so sorry," Ava said, pressing her hands to her chest.

An unexpected rush of heat washed over Zoey, sweat beading along her spine. "Sorry for what?" she asked, unsure she even wanted to know the answer.

"You don't know, do you?" Julie asked, her shoulders dropping, her voice breaking. "You haven't heard?"

On any given day around campus, there was some gossip running wild. Only this time, it felt personal. "Will someone tell me what's happened?"

"She doesn't know..." Ava breathed, her hand snapping out to hold Julie's arm.

Every warm space in Zoey's chest grew cold at the pity in their gazes. The world slowly dropped out from under her. "Please," she barely whispered. "What don't I know?"

Julie knelt next to her, placing a comforting hand on Zoey's leg. "I wish I wasn't the one to have to show you this." She pulled her phone from her pocket and hit a few buttons before handing Zoey the cell phone and adding, "I'm so sorry, Zoey."

One look at the screen, and Zoey's body begged to collapse in on itself. The campus faded around her. The view was all too familiar. The black dress she'd worn with the strappy sandals. The lace bra.

Every footstep walking by her sounded like thunder to her ears. Every laugh or word spoken was too loud. Her focus narrowed on the rip of her dress, her bare breasts, her legs spread wide, and her vagina on display for all to see. But worse than the image was the message: A PRETTY PIECE FROM NYU. WE DESTROYED HER. WHO WANTS HER NEXT?

Zoey's hand trembled as the phone slipped from her

hand. She looked into Ava's and Julie's slack expressions and wet, dull eyes before she heard the laughter and the voices. The fingers pointed her way. Some snickers and slurs. *Slut. Whore.* She recoiled, feeling each blow.

"Hey, sexy," a deep voice suddenly said from her right. A handsome face filled her vision, cold arrogance gleaming in steely brown eyes. "Busy tonight?"

Zoey's stomach roiled, and she fought against the chill stealing all the heat in her soul. She got up to run, to hide, to escape. But her legs gave out, the world disappearing around her as she threw up on his shoes.

CHAPTER 1

ONE YEAR LATER...

The streets of midtown Manhattan were foggy from the rain earlier in the day. Rhys Harrington breathed in the heavy night air as he strode up the stone steps of the ultra-exclusive, upscale sex club, Phoenix, shortly after nine o'clock. In the 1920s, the historic building located on 5th Avenue was a gentleman's cigar club. When Rhys bought the property and business ten years ago, he'd done so with another thought in mind. This corner piece of New York City, where anyone who stepped inside the doors left different than they came in, now housed fantasies and sexual delights.

Rhys wrapped his hand around the smooth golden handle and opened the heavy wooden door, entering the classy cigar lounge. Round tables were full of customers, enjoying a drink of fine bourbon and a cigar. Three bartenders dressed in tuxes served up drinks while waitresses and waiters tended to the customers at the tables. Rhys continued on, heading through the door at the back that led to his large office. His huge cherry-wood desk sat in the center, surrounded by bookcases and art he'd collected over the years. He moved to one of the bookcases, took off a book, and lifted the wood there. After he pressed his finger against the fingerprint reader, the bookcase began moving, revealing the hidden stairwell behind. He traveled down the staircase, surrounded by stone walls, as the cabinet sealed shut behind him.

When he reached the bottom, he opened another door, immediately greeting his longtime security detail. "Andre, how are things?"

Former military, Andre stood at the door, alert and ready. He smiled in greeting, warming his typically hard green eyes. He didn't hold a weapon; Andre *was* the weapon. Any threat walking through the door would regret their choices. "Can't complain, boss," Andre replied with a thick Texan accent.

"Then, it's a good night, indeed." Rhys headed past him, but stopped before he walked through the next door. "Let me know if any trouble comes up tonight."

"You know it," Andre said, inclining his head.

Every person on Rhys's payroll also got playtime at Phoenix. It kept his employees loyal, like family. They fought to protect this club and its members as much as Rhys did, and that kept everyone safe. When he entered the main area of Phoenix, he felt eyes turn to him, the pulsating energy in the room washing over him. The seating section had brown leather couches set around square coffee tables. The gas fireplace cast a romantic glow on the place, and the large, dim chandeliers over each table added to the warmth of the space. The women wore fine lingerie; the men were shirtless, wearing only black slacks. He recognized every face, even behind the masquerade masks. As the owner of Phoenix, he personally met everyone who applied for membership. Even the members who required anonymity and wore full-face masks, Rhys knew well. He knew every secret of every person in his club, and with that trust, he offered sexual freedom at a steep price. The level of security needed to keep an identity hidden determined the cost of the membership. With the tunnels from Prohibition beneath the building, members could enter from various locations across the city. The men and women working at the club were all retired military who understood the value of secrecy and honor.

Phoenix lived in a gray area when it came to the law. The rich, famous, and powerful paid to watch two consenting adults have sex in a show of their choosing. The men and women in that show were compensated for their participation. To Rhys, this was adults consenting to a mutually beneficial agreement. One that provided the client with a sexual fantasy they enjoyed watching, and offered financial payment to someone who wanted it. Everyone knew that money bought silence. In Rhys' experience, every person could be bought, for the right price.

Tonight, a quick sweep of his clientele told Rhys that four famous actors were there, along with their spouses, as well as a group of politicians, and a handful of Wall Street brokers. Rhys moved to the door off to the side of the bar that led to his office on this floor. The only other rooms down here were the private ones, where the nightly shows took place.

Before long, Rhys entered his office. The space had once been used to hold oak barrels full of whiskey, and some nights, Rhys swore he could catch that oaky scent lingering. When he stepped behind his desk in the stone-walled room and faced the two black leather client chairs in front of him, a low voice said, "You're late."

Rhys glance toward the doorway. Retired from the United States Navy SEALs Forces, Archer Westbrook entered the office and took a client chair. He had short and stylish brown hair, sharp features, and wise dark blue eyes. A friend from college with similar sexual tastes, Archer had been with Rhys from day one. Responding to Archer, Rhys glanced at his watch and grinned. "I've got five minutes." He shook out of his blazer, leaving it on his chair.

"You'll be ready in five?"

Rhys nodded. "Is Rigger's virgin here?"

"She is, ready and waiting." Archer interviewed, vetted, and handled finding participants for the shows.

Tonight was Senator Matthew Rigger's night. Part of having a Phoenix membership meant that one night a month, each client could pick their preferred pleasure. The only rule? You could watch, but not touch. Phoenix was for voyeurs. Rich and famous singles and couples, looking for shows to excite them. Couples typically partook in their own sexual play when the show was over and the crowd was gone from the room. Phoenix provided rooms just for that. A few times a month, Rhys let members partake in the shows. He hand-chose the members to allow anyone who wanted to participate a chance to explore a flesh-to-flesh experience. No fantasy was overlooked. All needs were catered to. Phoenix lived and breathed sex. But when virgins were requested, Rhys took control of the show. The responsibility was greater. The risks higher. The emotions deeper.

"I'll be out shortly," he told Archer. Not waiting for a response, Rhys headed into the adjoining bathroom. Wasting no time, he stripped and showered, and dried off just as quickly. When he returned to his office, he left his clothes off and opened the safe behind the painting on the wall. From there, he took out his sleek black masquerade mask.

After he slipped it on, he slid into his pressed black slacks from the closet and headed across the hallway. When he reached the door, he exhaled a long breath. Virgins were not his preference. He lived for lust, passion, and all that was in between. But he understood the responsibility of handling emotions and protecting the women who entered his club.

He took one more deep breath and focused on giving

Rigger the show he wanted while doing right by the virgin in his care. When he strode through the door, he found that most of the members had come into the playroom. Not unexpected. Rhys didn't partake in the shows often, and when he did, the members showed up. He knew why. People loved power. As the head of Phoenix and born into the wealthy Harrington family, he represented that.

The crowd stationed around the room silenced as he strode in, the door shutting behind him. This space was the size of a typical conference room, but surrounded by stone walls, flickering candles, and with a velvet chaise against the far wall, it felt intimate. Next to the chaise was a gold platter with a condom and a black silk robe resting on top. But none of that held his attention when he finally caught sight of the woman waiting for him. She stood next to the dark-purple velvet chaise. Behind her delicate mask, he saw light hazel eyes accentuated with soft makeup that led down to high cheekbones, a gentle nose, and burgundy-painted lips. All that delicate beauty was surrounded by long strawberry-blonde hair. Rhys couldn't stop his gaze from slowly traveling over her dark-green lingerie and garter belt all the way down to sexy black heels that made her legs look a mile long. By the time he reached her face again, his cock was hard, greedy.

He approached her, feeling the energy in the room tickling across his skin. When he stopped in front of her, he noted the heavy rise and fall of her chest. She had trouble holding his eye contact. And yet, she appeared to force herself to. Shy, but brave. A combination he hadn't known he liked until right now. She didn't once look away as he circled her, eyeing up his treat for the night. He tested her, stroking a finger down her arm, and the response she gave was immediate. Her cheeks flushed and lips parted, a slight tremble running through her. *Gorgeous.*

Heat flooded him as he made his way back in front of her and tucked a thumb under her chin, lifting her gaze to his. More to try to understand her than for the show, he stared into her eyes then dropped his mouth to hers. He kissed her, soft and gentle, showing her they were in no rush tonight. He had no plans to toss her onto the chaise and steal her virginity. No, with every slide of his tongue, he hoped she understood he'd have her begging before he dared take what she was willingly offering him tonight.

She gave a soft moan that had him moving forward, pulling her tighter against him, and deepening the kiss. He felt the crowd's eyes, sensed their stillness, and he embraced the spike of adrenaline burning through his veins. But when he heard the crowd shift, growing impatient, he realized how long he'd been kissing her, so he gave them what they wanted to see tonight.

He broke from her to step behind the woman. She shuddered when he unhooked her bra and dragged the lacy straps down her arms. Her breathy sigh slid over him as he cupped her small breasts and teased her rosy nipples. Unable to stop himself, he pressed his cock against her bottom, giving her a taste of what she'd soon have. What she'd soon beg him for. When she wiggled her hips encouragingly, he tucked his fingers into her panties and slid them down. Every moment slow, easy. For her. And for the crowd. He caught all the heated eyes on him, felt the burn of how much he liked that, and then he kissed her shoulder. He took her hand and guided her to the chaise.

Drawn into those gorgeous eyes of hers, he dropped his mouth onto hers before he picked her up and laid her out on the cushions. Right here, right now, he didn't give two fucks about the show anymore. Innocence and purity, waiting for him to take. But there was something unique about her, something that felt addictive.

He opened his pants, unable to take his eyes off her. While she watched him undress, her cheeks burned deeper, and he wondered, as his cock spilled free, how deep he could make those cheeks burn. She took in the size of him, and her wide eyes made him grin, a most unexpected reaction. Usually, he kept things all business. All pleasure. But with her...*what is it about you?*

He knew she expected him to cover her body and take her. Instead, he thrust his hands beneath her bottom and lifted her to his mouth. At the first gentle stroke of his tongue against her tight heat, her chin tilted up, a soft moan spilling out. A sound that tightened his groin. She tasted sweet as he slowly stroked over her clit, swirling the bud, until he dipped lower and groaned at her lovely wetness. She shuddered beneath him, and a quick look up at her revealed those cheeks were even darker than he'd hoped. Over and over again, he teased her, taking her right to the edge, then slowing down. Making her wild. When she gave a loud moan and a hard tremble, he lowered her bottom down to the chaise again then knelt in front of her. She reached for his arms then, holding him in such a way that felt far too intimate for the surroundings. It occurred to him that this woman was unlike anyone he'd met before. A virgin, shy, but also full of passion. The contradiction fascinated and intrigued him.

Unable to look away from her, he swiped his thumb over her clit. Her lips parted, and soft moans spilled out. A sound so beautiful, he accepted the invitation. He leaned over and kissed her as he stroked his fingers down her drenched folds. She tightened her lips on his when he slid one finger inside her tight heat and slowly worked her over. By the time he inserted another finger, her fingernails were digging into his arms. Not to stop him, but to bring him closer. Every swipe of her tongue against his was begging for him to take her where she'd never gone.

Tonight, he'd take her far past that.

Her breaths became heavy, her moans louder as she broke away from the kiss, her chin angling up. He was tempted to continue driving her wild with his fingers, but he knew better. She'd accept him easier on the edge of her pleasure. And with only her comfort and safety on his mind, he sheathed himself in the condom. He shifted closer, staying on his knees between her spread thighs. He became lost in the sweetness of her eyes. Something in her soul, keeping him transfixed. He only looked away to drench the tip of his cock in her arousal. Around him, he sensed the crowd go quiet, eager for what came next.

A whimper escaped her as he inserted just the tip, and he met her eyes. The crowd faded once again, and the most unexpected reaction overtook him. With a hand on her hip, he did what he'd never done with anyone to walk through Phoenix's doors; he cupped her face intimately and held her gaze, keeping her attention on him. Protecting her, shielding her, becoming absorbed in her. Lost in all the unexpected magic that silently passed between them, he thrust forward, her shocked gasp echoing around him. His eyes shut of their own accord at her tight heat squeezing him like a damn vise. A low groan spilled from his lips as he slowly pulled out, staring down at the blood of her innocence. He looked to her face again, but the heated eyes he expected to see weren't on him. Nor was her mask. Her bare face revealing hurt, hatred, and rage all directed at someone in the crowd. Then a single tear fell down her beautiful face, and a protective burn coursed through his veins while a haunting truth dawned on him.

This woman had an agenda tonight, and Rhys had played right into her plan.

CHAPTER 2

Zoey pushed past the pinch stealing her breath as the very innocence that had felt like a dark cloud over her life was finally broken. Oh, how much easier it would be to get lost in the masked man deep inside her. The sculpted lines of his face, squared jaw, jet-black hair, and gray eyes looked oddly familiar, but she couldn't place if, or where, she'd met him. Most of all, his touch felt *good*, so not what she had expected for tonight. It made no sense, but she'd swear she knew him and had kissed him a hundred times before now. Gorgeous and seductive, he oozed a passion she'd never known in her life. Like, if she allowed herself, she could let go, and his capable hands and strong, muscular body could take her places she'd never gone, and she'd be safe. But that delight was never meant for her. Only one thing had brought Zoey to Phoenix tonight. Justice. And even with their masks on, across the room, she knew the men who'd altered the direction of her life, Jake Grant and Scott Ross, were there, in attendance, watching her lose her virginity. When her lover for the night had withdrawn from her and she caught sight of the proof of her virginity, and knew everyone else did too, she had slid her mask off as accidentally as she could. Sweet revenge filled her when both Jake and Scott rose from their seats.

She let every emotion they'd made her feel for the last year show on her face. She nearly didn't do it. She threw up before the show and almost walked out twice. But she did it, and tonight, she'd leave all the pain, all the trauma, all of it, right there. Tomorrow was a new day, with new beginnings, where she wouldn't be stuck in a loop of the past. She could return to the old her. The shy her. The one who would never do something this bold. The woman who trusted blindly, who wanted to find love, who believed people were inherently good.

A soft swipe brushed across her face, and she realized the man hovering above her was touching her. Only then did she notice he was wiping away her tears. Some emotion appeared in his eyes, something protective and fierce. Something that made her feel oddly safe, even when she'd never been more exposed, both physically and emotionally. And that was the most unexpected reaction of all, that being watched, under this man's care, stole her timidity away. She'd expected to hate his touch, not to want more of him while a crowd watched, and she certainly hadn't expected to feel safe with him. She had a plan for tonight, but that plan was fading under his penetrating stare. The truth was as clear as it was surprising; she wanted *more.*

The masked man glanced over his shoulder, and she caught the narrowing of his eyes. She didn't need to look to know he saw Jake and Scott, maybe even noticed the paleness of their faces under their masks before they both left the room.

When his focus returned to her, there was a hard question in his eyes. It would go unanswered. She never planned on telling him, regardless of how much she wanted to beg him to keep going. She owed this man—any man—nothing. He obviously thought otherwise, since he dropped his mouth to her ear and said, "You will tell me the truth."

She never got to respond. He dropped a kiss on her mouth that stole every single thought right out of her head. All the heat that had vanished was back with the intensity of his kiss. With each powerful move of sheer seduction, she began to forget. Forget why she'd come there tonight. Why she'd spent the last year tracking Jake's and Scott's emails and text messages to find a way to get justice. To prove to them, and herself, that she was not the whore they'd made her out to be. That she was, until a moment ago, a virgin. And that they never broke her. That she could be this bold, this brave, and that no matter what they had done, they didn't destroy her.

No matter what everyone on campus thought, she knew the truth. And now they did too.

The masked man's mouth moved with intent, his finger stroking over her clit until her eyes rolled back into her head from the hot pleasure. His kisses and sizzling touches were beyond anything she'd ever experienced before. They weren't to take; they were to give. Obviously, he enjoyed pleasuring a woman, and she'd never felt so wanted, so beautiful...all the things she'd never felt before in her life. A sudden gasp was pulled from deep in her chest when he took hold of her knee, sliding it up a little as he shifted his hips. His cock felt impossibly huge, stretching her until a whimper escaped her mouth.

The noise only made him deepen his kiss. Then his mouth slid to her neck, her breast, her nipple, sucking and playing until her body was lit up. Every touch rocked through her and to her core. Every stroke tickled in all the right places. His body felt like a beacon of light, and she felt consumed by the warmth of him.

She sensed the crowd watching, but she couldn't find shame. In fact, she liked that she held their attention. That she was the reason they were likely turned on. That they were enamored by her. The masked man broke the kiss with a low groan that rumbled in her belly, and he cupped her face. Holding her pinned, he moved faster, and the pleasure…oh, the pleasure was endless, making her curl her toes and arch her back. But she wasn't meant to enjoy this, to *need* this, to fully let go. She bit her lip, struggling against where he took her, not wanting to give him everything.

His fingers tightened in her hair. A low growl rumbled beside her ear. "Don't fight me."

She snapped her eyes open to his burning gaze beneath his mask. Trapped in the power of that stare and enduring thrusts that sent never-ending pleasure coursing into every molecule of her body, her breath hitched. He drove in harder and grinned when she shuddered.

He brought his mouth close to hers then nipped her lip. "That's right, sweetheart, give me what I want."

What happened next was completely unexpected. He thrust once, hard enough to make her scream again, and any pleasure she thought she'd had before this moment, was incomparable to the sheer force that stormed over. Wave after wave of penetrating euphoria blasted across her senses until there was no man, no crowd, no Phoenix, only the intensity erupting deep in her soul.

Sometime later, a round of applause forced her to reopen her eyes. She wiggled her toes, but her legs were heavy. Far too heavy to move. She found herself staring into the masked man's gorgeous eyes, his softer cock still buried deep inside her. Her first surprise was that the fire in his gaze hadn't lessened. The second was that the protectiveness she felt emanating from him seemed stronger now.

Tonight, she did what she'd planned to do, and suddenly,

the weight of the last year slammed into her. Her throat squeezed and chin quivered. The masked man above her held her stare, almost like he knew she was about to break apart, and yet, he didn't look bothered. No, he looked...*ready.*

"Breathe," he told her gently.

She let out the air stuck in her tight throat. A moment later, the crowd began to leave the room, talking and laughing like they hadn't just witnessed her having sex for the first time. Maybe this was normal for them, but it certainly wasn't normal for her. And with Jake and Scott gone, her heart had a moment to ask...*what did you just do?*

When she heard the door click shut, the masked man, still deep inside her, did the most unexpected thing. He gathered her in his arms until she was sitting on him, and then he put a hand on the back of her head to hold her close.

He said absolutely nothing, but his hold tightened, and the warmth he exuded shattered something inside of her.

The tears she'd fought broke free. The pain of a year, spilling out. The loss of her dreams, of what never was, emptying into this stranger's arms.

Only when her tears dried did he shift and cup her face intimately. He held her stare like he owed her something. And then he gently kissed her, almost like a thank you for what she'd given him. She became just as lost as she'd been before. Taken to a place where her heart could nearly believe all men weren't bad.

When he finally broke the kiss, he lifted her until he set her on her feet. She felt the heat of her blush rush over her cheeks, now reminded she was naked and not nearly as brave as she'd portrayed earlier tonight. He grabbed the black silk robe from the tray and dressed her. With a gentle look in his eyes, he fastened the robe and said, "I'll give you a moment. Then I expect to hear exactly who you are and what the hell game you were playing tonight."

Instead of lying, since she was never very good at that, she simply nodded. Naked, with the full condom still wrapped around his gorgeous cock, she watched him leave, his solid, muscled ass and flexing back, holding her full attention. How easy it would be to believe men could be good. That she could trust them. But men lied. They destroyed lives. She didn't owe any man a damn thing, certainly not a stranger who thought she owed him her pain.

CHAPTER 3

*W*hen Rhys returned home later that evening, hot irritation licked through his veins. After dressing at the end of the show, he'd returned to talk with the woman he learned from Archer was named Zoey Parker, only to discover that she'd snuck out and took off. Rhys lived by strict rules. It kept Phoenix safe. He only slept with a woman once. No star appeared multiple times at the club. Only members were allowed in the building, except for the stars of the show, who went through Archer's grueling vetting process. And finally, Rhys didn't ask for any personal information about his stars. He didn't know the names of the women he slept with. He kept things strictly professional. Zoey had him breaking his ironclad rules, and that didn't sit well.

To rid himself of his mood, he showered off his frustration and prepared his house for poker night. He lived on the Lower East Side, enjoying the energy of the neighborhood. The trendy bars, nightclubs, and music venues gave him life when he needed it after Katherine, his college sweetheart, passed away from cancer. While his income had grown substantially since he bought the one-bedroom condo ten years ago, he never felt the urge to move. But he had done some renovations, adding modern gray slate kitchen cabinets. An up-and-coming painter had created a woman's face on the kitchen wall in black and white. Her eyes had always looked haunted to Rhys. He realized now that he'd seen those eyes earlier. Zoey's eyes were the same, and he couldn't get them out of his head.

The large room was furnished with a mustard-colored couch and chrome tables. The back wall was all glass from floor to ceiling, offering a gorgeous view of Manhattan, the city lights glowing as bright as ever. To the right of that glass was a door leading to his rooftop patio, the original reason he'd bought the property. Ten years ago, there were tiny trees and plants there. Now his pool, hot tub, and sitting area could beat any park in New York City.

When he reached for beers in the fridge, there was a knock on the door. It opened a moment later, and his good friend, Kieran Black, a firefighter with the New York City Fire Department, entered. He had dirty-blond hair and strong green eyes that were both trusting and warm. His lean body came from hours of training for the Ironman Triathlon. Kieran took one look at Rhys' face and asked, "Who do I need to kill?"

Beers in hand, Rhys shut the fridge and snorted. "You're too good to kill anyone for me."

Beside Kieran, Hunt Walker, a homicide detective for the New York Police Department, grinned sheepishly. "But I'm not. How do you want them dead, slow with a knife or fast with a gun?" His light-brown eyes held a slightly harder edge, like he'd seen things that would break most people. His tall and muscular physique intimated grown men. His messy golden-brown hair gave the appearance that he was easygoing, and typically, he was.

Kieran and Hunt were lifelong friends. Rhys had met them through his sexual interludes at private parties during college, as with Archer, and the friendship stuck. Brothers, not by blood but something deeper. A tight connection that remained important in Rhys' life. And along with Archer, both men often partook in the shows at Phoenix.

"While I thank you for the offer to kill someone for me," Rhys muttered. "It's not necessary. We had a situation tonight at the show."

Of course, Hunt missed nothing. As he took a seat at the poker table set up in Rhys' living room, he asked, "Archer missed something in vetting that virgin?"

Rhys placed the beers in the cup holders. "That's what I'm waiting to find out."

Kieran dropped down into his usual spot across from Rhys. "That's unlike Archer to miss anything. What happened?"

Rhys took his seat and cracked open his beer. "This woman, Zoey, took off her mask and showed her face to two members, who left the moment they saw her."

At that, Hunt straightened in his seat. "She identified herself on purpose?"

Rhys acknowledged that frustrating realization with a heavy nod. "I've got Archer looking into her and what fucking game she was playing."

"Damn," Kieran breathed. "I pity her, then."

Before Rhys could reply, another knock came at the door. Archer strode in, his jaw set. "Sorry I'm late," he said by way of greeting.

Every Friday night was poker night. The game had been long-standing, with luck usually landing on Kieran's side, who now said to Archer, "For your tardiness, you're throwing an extra hundred into the pot."

As cool as always, Archer grabbed his beer, cracked it

open, and took a long gulp. "Rhys can toss that cash in. He's the one making me hunt down information from a year ago."

No secrets were held between Rhys and his chosen family. They were his sounding board, his confidants in his world of so many secrets, the only people Rhys trusted. He shuffled the deck of cards and nodded Archer on. "Let's hear what you found."

"As you know, the woman is Zoey Parker," Archer reported, taking his seat at the table. "In college, she got drunk at a party, and two frat fools took a picture of her naked. I got hold of it." The long pause that followed said enough about what type of photograph it was, but Archer added anyway, "It's explicit."

Rhys didn't like where this was going. "All right, go on."

Archer set his beer back in the cup holder on the poker table. "From what I discovered, rumors about her being a slut, a whore, trash—any name you can think of—spread like wildfire throughout the campus. She was bullied for the final two months of school, and it was bad. Most of the things in that file came from old social media posts."

Hunt asked, "Which is why you didn't find this out during vetting?"

Archer's jaw muscles clenched twice. Then he nodded. "This situation is unusual. Her profile is gone now, so her name wasn't linked to the social media post, which is why it didn't show up in my background check. Zoey never reported the incident to the NYPD or the college police, so there's no paperwork on her assault."

"Wonder why that is," Kieran murmured.

Rhys wondered that himself. He began handing out the cards. "What was she in school for?"

"Biological science. She got that degree. But it looks like she had originally planned to attend vet school at Colorado State University. She was accepted but turned it down.

Now she works at a veterinary clinic as a groomer in Brooklyn."

When Rhys finished dealing, he lifted his cards and began putting them in order. "Any information come up about her mental health?"

Archer organized his cards then set them down. "She went to therapy for six months—that's all I could find without going any deeper. To get the actual records, it would cost you some cash." Archer had a couple of hackers in his pocket. "But she's not on any medication or had any arrests. From the way it looks, she lives a very quiet life with a couple roommates." Another long stretch of silence settled in as Archer's lips thinned. "Something came up that you're not going to like."

Rhys arched an eyebrow. "What's that?"

"The two men who took the photograph are Phoenix members."

"Oh, shit," Kieran drawled.

Hunt snorted a laugh. "Not for long."

That explained why the men had run out. "Who were they?" Rhys had been too enthralled by Zoey to notice anything but the back of their heads as they were leaving.

"Scott Ross and Jake Grant."

Both were hotshots on Wall Street.

At Rhys' frown, Archer asked, "What do you want me to do?"

"Dig deeper."

"Into Zoey?"

Rhys shook his head. Anything else he learned, he wanted to come from her mouth. "Into Scott and Jake. Get me a solid file on them and what happened that night."

Archer lifted his eyebrows. "And Zoey?"

"Let me think on her." He never reacted quickly, not with anyone who walked through Phoenix's doors. He had a responsibility to those who trusted him to fulfill their fantasies and to keep them safe while doing so. With Zoey, the situation was different. He felt responsible for her. But he needed to think over his reaction to her. She'd gotten what she wanted and likely wasn't a threat to his members. He should leave it at that and walk away. But why didn't he want to?

He grabbed a hundred dollars' worth of poker chips and tossed them Archer's way. "For now, prepare to get your asses handed to you."

"Keep dreaming, Harrington," Hunt drawled as laughter blew apart the tension.

* * *

WHEN ZOEY MADE it home after sneaking out of Phoenix, her hands were still shaking. Standing outside the black-painted front door of her loft, she looked at the cashier's check again: ZOEY PARKER. $100,000.00 signed by Rhys Harrington. She folded the paper, shoved it back into her purse, and shut her eyes. She'd never seen that much money before and never imagined earning money from selling her virginity. But after all she'd been through, there was no guilt, no shame, only freedom from her pain. With the money from the show, she could put a down payment on a house back home, where homes were a fraction of the price in Brooklyn. The plan was to turn the main floor of the house into a grooming shop. Sure, that dream was a long cry from becoming a veterinary, but she'd grown to love her job and being around animals. And the truth was, she missed home. It took everything she had to graduate undergrad. The last two months of school had been long and torturous. She still wasn't sure what it said about her that she hadn't told her parents the truth about why she gave up her dream of vet school. That being burned-out wasn't the reason at all. She also hadn't admitted that she avoided going home the last year because she couldn't face them, not with the complete failure her life had become. Both her parents were doctors. Mom, a family doctor. Dad, a vascular surgeon. While they offered support, she could hear the disappointment in their voices. She couldn't bear to see it on their face too.

But that was then, and this was now. She felt ready to face them. The weight of a year of pain felt gone from her shoulders. She'd worked hard to turn everything around. And was proud of what she'd accomplished. She lived in a roomy loft on Brooklyn's waterfront with her two roommates. On the southern edge of the Brooklyn Navy Yard, in an old warehouse, they rented the place for a ridiculous amount of money that none of them could afford on their own. The large windows provided beautiful natural light, and the openness was what had made her fall in love with the apartment in the first place. The distance from Manhattan was the second. Her night at Phoenix was the first time Zoey had returned to Manhattan since her last day of school. She threw up the second she got off the subway, and stayed close to total strangers so she wouldn't have to walk the streets alone.

When Zoey finally unlocked the door and strode inside, her roommate Hazel Rose immediately leapt up from the couch, nearly plowing into Zoey. "What happened? Tell me every single detail." Hazel had medium-length light-brown hair and beautiful light-blue eyes, and the longest natural eyelashes Zoey had ever seen on anyone.

Zoey snorted a laugh. "Well, I'll tell you what happened if you let me shut the door."

"Oh, sorry." Hazel smiled sheepishly, releasing her tight hold on Zoey's arms.

Their other roommate, Elise Fanning, smiled from the

couch. "I had to take her jogging to get her to finally sit down." Elise had long dark-brown hair and strong dark-brown eyes, and she lounged on the sofa like she didn't have a worry in the world.

Zoey always envied that about Elise, and she'd counted on Elise's calm nature many, *many* times. Zoey had met them when she saw the wanted ad for a roommate on a coffee shop's community board after the assault. The rest was history, and now Hazel and Elise felt more like sisters than friends.

"I wouldn't get too excited," said Zoey, kicking off her heels and plopping into the chair across from Elise. "I had sex."

Hazel rolled her eyes at Elise. "She had sex." Her gaze fell to Zoey, and she waved her on. "In a room full of people. Oh my God, Zoey, tell me *everything*."

Again, Zoey laughed. "I don't really know what to say. It's just as you'd imagine it to be. Rich, luxurious atmosphere. Everyone wears masks, which honestly, made things less scary."

"So, it wasn't creepy?" Elise asked.

"Surprisingly, not creepy," Zoey replied after a moment's thought. "Actually, very sensual. Like the room was vibrating with lust. It's like there is no judgment there. Just a connection to watch others." She was sure she wasn't getting it right, so she shrugged. "It's hard to explain. It's just…not creepy… It's sexy as hell, and I shockingly liked it."

Hazel sat next to Elise, leaning forward. "And did you take off your mask? Did Jake and Scott see you?"

Zoey nodded. "Even behind the masks, I knew who they were." Their faces were burned into her mind.

"And?" Elise pressed. "What happened?"

"They took one look at me, lost all the color in their faces, and left."

"Fucking cowards," Elise snapped.

"Wow," Hazel breathed, leaning back against the couch, hands pressed to her chest. "That must have been empowering for you."

Zoey thought it over and finally nodded. "I think it was the biggest fuck you I could have given them. That I knew, and they knew and saw, that the lies they spread were never true. That I was a virgin up until tonight. And that they didn't break me or make me afraid of them. I've already been in front of people, exposed completely, and that was not my choice. This was my choice. On *my* terms."

Elise gave a firm nod. "Good for you. Fucking pricks."

Zoey smiled. "My sentiments exactly."

Hazel bounced on the couch. "So, what happened after that?"

"The virginity-taker slid the mask back on my face and whispered in my ear that I owed him answers."

Elise's brows shot up. "Did you give him those answers?"

"Nope, I snuck out before anyone could question me."

"Atta girl." Elise grinned.

Hazel shook her head slowly as if she couldn't believe any of this was true. "Wait. What was the guy like?"

Zoey dropped her head back and shut her eyes, swearing she could still feel his breath by her ear, his hands on her body, his cock deep inside her. "Incredible," she breathed, glancing back to her friends. "I've never met anyone like him. He was so passionate. I didn't know a touch could feel like that."

"Wow," Hazel said again, eyes twinkling. "Well, as far as losing-your-virginity stories go, yours wins, every time."

Zoey nodded with a smile. "Maybe an unconventional way to lose your virginity, but he definitely made the experience memorable. I wasn't really expecting him to care about my needs; I just figured he'd want to put on a show."

"But it wasn't like that?" Elise asked.

Zoey shook her head. "He was just tuned into me. Does that make sense?"

"Total sense," Elise agreed with a smile.

Zoey grabbed some chips out of the bowl on the coffee table, tossing them into her mouth as Hazel asked, "Did they ask you how you found out about the place?"

She finished chewing then answered, "No, they have nothing more than what I put on the application." In which, she said she'd heard about the club from a member. In actuality, Hazel was a reporter and had gotten wind of the secret sex club in Manhattan.

"Did they have any idea that I hacked in to get that code?" Elise asked.

"None," Zoey replied.

Elise owned a private investigation company, which was how they'd learned about the financial gift that came along with doing the show. But she'd also obtained the necessary code to access Phoenix's portal through the cigar club's website. After Zoey entered the code, it brought her to the application with the required photographs and intimate details about her life.

The conversation about Zoey applying to Phoenix to confront Jake and Scott didn't happen all at once. It was a handful of conversations and lots of late-night thoughts. Both Elise and Hazel had been there for Zoey after she graduated and began trying to bandage her life back together again. Two strangers had been her shelter through a fierce storm. Ava and Julie had moved back to their hometowns, and the communication grew silent after that. Zoey hadn't spoken to them in over six months. She'd never forget what Elise and Hazel did for her, picking up all her broken pieces until she resembled a human again. But one night, after a first date ended with Zoey having a panic attack, she decided this was her way out. Her do-over.

"Well, I'm glad they didn't suspect anything," Elise commented, grabbing some chips out of the bowl. "The last thing I need is Rhys Harrington coming after me."

Zoey nodded. "Yeah, no kidding." From what she read up on the owner online, he was the CEO of Harrington Finance before he stepped down when he bought the cigar club. The New York City Harringtons were a wealthy family, coming from old money, and were very powerful.

"So, you're in the clear?" Hazel asked. "All this is over? You can finally move home and start fresh?"

Like a world of pain had suddenly been shed from her skin, Zoey smiled, feeling more honest than she had in a year. "It's done. Over." A sudden, unexpected lump formed in her chest, but she cleared her throat and pushed past it. "I can finally move home."

At whatever crossed Zoey's face, Elise cocked her head. "That's good, right?"

Again, Zoey smiled, only this time, it didn't feel so honest. "It's good."

"I'm just so happy for you," Hazel said, still bouncing on the couch. "And so proud of you." She jumped up and all but threw herself at Zoey again, hugging her tightly. "That took some balls, to do what you did tonight."

"I couldn't have done it without you," Zoey said, resting her chin on Hazel's shoulder. "Without either of you."

Elise gave a rare soft smile from across the room. "That's why we're here, babe. We got you."

And this...*this* was good too.

CHAPTER 4

*L*ate into the next afternoon, Zoey was covered head-to-toe in dark-colored dog hair. The veterinary office always smelled somewhere between wet dog and sanitizer, and she never could get it out of her nose. And now, with Charlie, the big brown Labrador on her grooming table getting a blowout, her nose was also covered with fur. The dog pressed his head against Zoey's chest as she finished up drying him. By the time she was done, Charlie was wagging his tail and he had his tongue out in the biggest smile she'd ever seen on a dog. She kissed his nose. "Yes, you are the most handsome boy in the whole wide world."

He wagged his butt at her.

"And you know it too, don't you?" She laughed, helped him jump onto the stool, and then down onto the floor, and waited for him to stop his dancing before she reattached his leash and opened the door. Charlie went full steam toward the waiting room, promptly yanking himself out of Zoey's hold.

His owner caught the leash and reined the dog in with a laugh. "Was he a good boy?"

"Always a fantastic boy," Zoey said, finally reaching them.

Patty, Charlie's owner, stroked the dog's head and gave Zoey a curious look. "Any chance you've changed your mind on moving away?"

"No, sorry," Zoey said, aware that, like with last night's lump in her throat, her chest tightened whenever this subject came up. "Sadly, this is our last appointment, but have no worries at all. The lady replacing me is amazing." Well, Zoey thought so. She'd only met her replacement once, but she seemed friendly.

Patty gave a heavy sigh, still patting Charlie on the head. "Well, if you ask Charlie and me, no one can replace you, but we wish you the absolute best."

"Thanks, Patty." Zoey gave her a quick hug and Charlie another kiss on the head before they headed off to the receptionist, Betty, to pay their bill. Moving away from Brooklyn would be hard. She really did love her job and her clients. Most of all, she wasn't quite sure how she could live without Hazel and Elise. But Manhattan was too close, a harsh reminder of the NYU days she hadn't been able to escape. She needed freedom from the pain. She wanted to be the woman who wanted love, who wanted children, who wanted that quiet life. All she had to do was find her again.

She returned to her room and set to cleaning it up to leave for the day. Charlie had been her last appointment, and tonight was a girls' night. She quickly rinsed off, changed into skinny jeans, a black blouse, and black heels in the adjoining bathroom, and applied some darker makeup, throwing her hair up in a messy high ponytail before she left the room, shutting the door behind her.

"Have an awesome weekend, Betty," she called as she headed for the door. "I'll see you on Monday."

"Bye, sweetie." Betty gave a quick wave before turning back to her monitor.

Zoey focused on the front door again, noting how different she felt than the last time she'd left work. Stronger, maybe. Sexier, for sure. The shy girl from Sacramento had had sex in the most exclusive sex club in New York City. She laughed and shook her head to herself. Even she had a hard time believing it.

When she took a step outside, into the early evening, she nearly tripped at seeing Phoenix's head of security, Archer, leaning against a big black truck. He was the one who'd interviewed her and met her on the night of the show. She'd liked him then. It worried her that he was here now.

He gave a lopsided grin. "I'm sorry if I've surprised you."

She gathered herself enough not to stumble and hurried to his side, a million questions rushing through her mind. "Is everything okay?" she asked.

"Yes, of course," Archer said with a soft smile she was sure was meant to reassure her. It didn't work. As if he knew that, his voice softened. "Rhys would like to see you again and requests I bring you to Phoenix." He hesitated. Then his expression went utterly gentle, which on a face with such striking features looked pretty dreamy. "Believe me, Rhys only wants to have the talk he requested last night. Nothing to worry about."

"Ah…" She blinked, processed, and then managed, "Hold on a second. The man I was with last night was Rhys Harrington, the owner of Phoenix?"

Archer smirked. "Yes."

She had to pick her jaw off the ground. What in the holy hell? She thought the masked man had been some random guy. Albeit, she didn't know the ins and outs of the sex club. "Does Rhys always do the shows?"

"Not always, no," Archer explained, his thumbs tucked into the pockets of his jeans. "But he always handles any sensitive ones, so he knows everything is being done correctly."

Like a woman offering up her virginity, apparently.

Zoey blinked. Again. "Am I in trouble?"

Archer laughed softly. "No. Why would you be in trouble?"

Ah, because my best friend hacked into your security system and I manipulated and lied my way into a very private club.

Archer watched her thoughts play out on her face before he offered, "Let me give you a piece of advice. I have known Rhys for a very long time; when he says he wants to talk to you, it's not a suggestion. You either come now, or he'll come to you later. Trust me on that." Archer moved to the passenger-side door and opened it. "If it makes you feel better, there are security cameras there." He pointed above the clinic's door. "And there." He gestured across the street. "There's evidence you are with me. But also, text your roommates, let them know you are going to the cigar club and who you are going with. Let them know I'll bring you home after, I promise." He reached into his back pocket and pulled out his drivers' license from his wallet. "Take a picture and send it to your friends."

From the first time she met Archer, he'd done everything and anything to make her feel safe and comfortable. And the truth was, she did. "Okay," she said, reaching into her purse. She took the photo then fired off a text to the girls in their group chat.

I'll meet you at the restaurant tonight. Rhys Harrington wants to see me. I'm going to the cigar club now.

Elise's text came in an instant. Are you in trouble?

Don't think so. I'm with Archer, the head of security at Phoenix. Here's his ID. I'll call if I need you.

Yes, do!

33

Hazel's message popped up. WHAT? HOLY SHIT? RHYS-FUCKING-HARRINGTON? WHAT'S HAPPENING? OMG, I NEED TO KNOW EVERYTHING!!

Zoey chuckled and tucked her phone away. Poor Hazel was going to be a mess until Zoey figured out what in the hell was going on. She glanced up at Archer and gave a soft smile. "We're good."

"Excellent. Hop on in." He gestured her inside.

In minutes, they were on the road. The drive into Manhattan took longer than normal due to rush-hour traffic, but Archer's small talk made her feel comfortable. Until they crossed from Brooklyn into Manhattan, when her stomach roiled and a hot flash rushed across her, leaving her back sweaty against the seat. She knew it was irrational. That Brooklyn wasn't any safer than Manhattan. But Brooklyn *felt* safer; it was free of Scott and Jake.

"You're safe, Zoey. Just breathe."

She released the breath she was holding, not knowing she'd been holding it. She brushed it off with a laugh. "Sorry about that. I'm good."

Archer watched her closely and then gave her a firm nod before focusing back on the road.

She hated what this city did to her. The fear it created. She settled back into her seat.

When he finally parked at the curb and led her through the front door, her curiosity grew tenfold. The cigar club was lavish. Rhys' wealth showed here. Fabrics were luxurious, antique furniture even more so, no expense was spared with the design. And she was pretty sure the intricate gold fleurs on the bar were real. The place was busy, most tables full of customers drinking dark liquored alcohol, thick cigar smoke lingering in the air, an oddly pleasing aroma of cedar mixed with a pungent scent of tobacco. Amazing, considering the laws in the city banned smoking indoors. Which, of course, only told her that, when it came to Rhys Harrington, rules didn't necessarily apply.

She kept silent and followed Archer down a long hallway and through another door. Then her steps faltered at the view unfolding before her. Behind a one-way mirror, in what appeared to be a private room with whiskey barrels lining the stone walls, Scott and Jake sat on brown leather couches beside each other. They sipped bourbon, smoked cigars, and chit-chatted with Rhys sitting across from them. She recognized him immediately and chided herself for not noticing it the night they were together. She'd seen pictures of him on the Internet when Elise had researched Phoenix. Even if he was the most gorgeous man she'd ever seen in her life, with a body of sculpted muscles, a chiseled jawline, and a mesmerizing presence that demanded she continue to stare at him, her stomach dropped. "What the hell is this?" she snapped, whirling on Archer.

"You're safe," Archer said, holding up his hands nonthreateningly. "You've got a choice here. I can take you home right now. Or you can watch Rhys deal with them. He thought you'd appreciate the latter." Archer's expression showed only kindness and strength as he added, "Let Rhys right this wrong in the way he can. These bastards deserve far worse."

He's going to right a wrong? Her head spun as she moved closer to the one-way mirror. She stared at the two men who'd ruined her life. Destroyed her in ways she never thought anyone could destroy her. Beside her, she saw Archer fire off a text, and she noticed Rhys glancing at his phone.

His gaze lifted to the one-way mirror, and she felt the power of that stare like a punch to her stomach, knocking the wind right out of her. She was sure he couldn't see her, but it seemed like he was looking right at her, reminding her how last night had felt. To hold this man's attention was something powerful. Something addictive. Something profound. Rhys gave a slight nod, approval shining in his eyes. Then his gaze hardened when he looked at Scott and Jake. "I have no doubt you're wondering why I've asked you here," he said, picking up a file. "Explain this to me." He slid a photo across the coffee table between them.

One look at the paper, and Scott went ghostly white. Jake snorted and leaned back in his chair, crossing his arms. Zoey didn't know what had truly happened that awful night, but their reactions now made her believe that Jake was the leader, and Scott had followed. She couldn't help but wonder what would have happened if Scott, obviously a guy with a smidgen of a conscience, hadn't been there.

"Hot chick," Jake said. "Should I know her?"

Something deadly flashed across Rhys' expression. He arched a very slow and deliberate eyebrow. "Try again."

Jake averted his gaze.

Scott bowed his head.

Rhys grabbed the photo and tossed it aside like he couldn't stand to touch it before addressing them again. "Let me explain the situation to you. When we ran our background check on the woman in our show last night, this photograph came up."

Jake shifted in his seat.

Scott had yet to look up.

Rhys continued, "Of course, we put this photograph through a ruthless investigation after we discovered the woman did not give her consent. I don't think I need to tell you that, at the end of the investigation, your names were at the forefront. Do you care to explain that?"

Scott finally looked up. His skin ashen. "It's not how it looks."

"How it looks?" Rhys growled, his knuckles turning

white around his bourbon glass. "It looks like you drugged a young woman, photographed her, then blasted lies on social media."

"We didn't rape her," Jake said.

A vein protruded in the center of Rhys' forehead as he said in a very controlled voice, "You destroyed her life. How can you possibly believe that is any less of a crime than if you had raped her?"

Something broke inside of Zoey, something raw and unexpected, flooding her with emotions she couldn't control. Never had anyone spoken up for her like this. Even Ava and Julie had kept quiet, hiding behind her embarrassment and shame. Zoey had never let anyone in, never believed anyone would fight for her, and a bleeding spot in her heart needed this. She began shaking and couldn't stop, wrapping her arms around herself tightly.

Archer was there, squatting next to her, but never reaching to touch her. "Tell me you want to leave, and we leave. It's that simple, Zoey. What do you want to do?"

"No, I'm okay," she said, wiping at the moisture on her face with shaky hands. "I want to stay."

"Please look at me."

She turned her head, meeting Archer's concerned eyes. He gently said, "If that changes, tell me."

"Okay, yes, thank you." His kindness and trusting nature, Rhys' strength and protection, she felt it all wrap around her like a warm blanket. She looked back at the men who'd altered her life is such a dramatic way. The men who were complete opposites of these two strangers. But she knew the control Scott and Jake had over her. She didn't even know the woman she had been before that night anymore. The one who believed people were kind. The woman who trusted her own judgment. The one who thought bad things couldn't happen to her.

Jake finally lifted his head and snorted. "Rhys, is this going somewhere?"

Rhys grinned as he gestured at the one-way mirror. There was nothing friendly about it. "I've brought Zoey here to watch this."

Both men glanced at the window, shock on their faces. But Scott didn't look away.

"And the point?" Jake asked, entitled arrogance dripping off his voice.

"Your time in Phoenix is done," Rhys stated, matter of fact. "Your memberships revoked. I've recorded this conversation, and I'm giving the recording and the casefile to Zoey. The choice if she wants to have you prosecuted is her own." He leaned in, and Zoey had never seen anyone look so scary and sexy all at once. "Let me be very clear: stay away from her. Not a phone call. Not a house visit. Do not push me where it comes to her." Rhys lifted his glass to his mouth, and before taking a sip, he dismissed them. "Now get the fuck out."

Both men rose. Jake was out the door in less time it took Zoey to draw in a shaky breath.

Scott took a step out but stopped before exiting. He glanced at the window, heavy regret on his features. "I'm sorry, Zoey. I know that will never make up for my part in what I did to you, but I am. I'm just so sorry."

The emotion Zoey had been fighting burst wide open as Scott left. Like floodgates she couldn't keep shut, she dropped her head into her hands and cried. Sobbed for everything that had happened. For all the lies spread. For her squashed dreams. For Scott and Jake finally being held accountable. Most of all, she cried because it had happened in the first place. But when a warm, woodsy musk infused the air, she realized someone else had entered the room. Firm hands gathered her, and she was hoisted into strong arms as Rhys sat down, pulling her to straddle his waist.

He held her.

Truly held her.

Like he had last night.

And she let him, emptying her pain into this man's arms…a man who owed her nothing.

She had no idea how much time had passed before she lifted her head, not caring if her makeup was running down her face. She met Rhys' smoky gray eyes, transfixed by the strength in them.

He held up a USB stick. "For you."

"What's this?" she asked, accepting it.

"That is your evidence if you choose to seek justice against them."

She glanced at the USB stick. "But wouldn't that expose the club?"

His soft voice drew her gaze back up to meet a face so gorgeous she didn't think it could be real. "Sometimes, Zoey, telling the truth is worth the risk. This is one of those times. What was done to you was wrong. Scott and Jake should be brought to justice for that." He closed her hand with his, keeping the USB stick tight in her grip. "Take it. You decide what to do with it."

She held his gaze, and it felt oddly easy to do that. "For a year, I have believed the very worst in people. That no one can be trusted. That you can't believe a word anyone says, because people do terrible things. But this…you and Archer…" Her voice hitched, but she forced the words out to prove to herself that she didn't need to hide anymore. "I can't help but think that maybe hope's not all lost and that there really are good people out there."

"None of this should have happened to you." He wiped a fallen tear like it was his duty to do so. When he dropped his hand, holding her intimately against him, he asked, "Would it be all right if I drive you back home?"

She inhaled and exhaled deeply, pulling back emotions she had become an expert at hiding. "Thank you, but I'm okay. I'm actually meeting up with my roommates tonight." To celebrate leaving her old life behind and stepping into this new one, where Manhattan didn't terrify her. "I'll make my way home with them after. Honestly, after all that, I could use the air. It's not far from here. I'll just walk." Of course, she'd call a taxi, but he didn't need to know that.

Not taking no for an answer, he rose with her in his arms and set her down on her feet. "Then, let me walk you." At her silence, he offered his hand, arching an eyebrow, which softened his strong features. "Indulge me, Zoey. It's a beautiful night."

There were a thousand reasons to say no. But she realized she didn't want to. She slid her hand into his. "You're right, it is a beautiful night."

CHAPTER 5

On any given day, Rhys could look a person in the eye and tell what their greatest desire was. He'd learned how to read people a long time ago. However, he realized on his walk through Central Park with Zoey that part of her allure was the mystery behind her. All the secrets Rhys had yet to discover, and how exactly she'd pulled off something he never thought possible. She was brave, but cautious. He noticed when they began walking that her gaze was darting, searching for any threats. Her posture was tense, ready. He liked how, fifteen minutes later, she smiled more, laughed a bit, and her shoulders lowered.

Along the path hugged by mature trees, Rhys gestured at an empty bench. "Come sit with me a moment." At the curious tilt of her head, he smiled gently. "I'd like to talk a minute, if that's all right with you."

She took her phone from her purse, glancing at the screen. "Let me just text my roommates that I'll be a few more minutes."

He waited for her to fire off the message before gesturing at the bench again. After she sat, he joined her. Knowing he needed to take this slowly and gently, he leaned forward, resting his elbows on his knees, but turned his head toward her. "You owe me no explanation, but I'd like to hear your truth."

"About what happened that night with Jake and Scott?" At Rhys' nod, she asked, "Why are you so interested?"

Why, indeed? "Because your story is the only one that matters here," he told her.

She breathed in and out slowly, turning away from him, staring out at nothing. But even from a side glance, the weight of her pain rested heavily on her face. "I wasn't really a party girl in college, but two months before I graduated, my old college friends talked me into going to a frat party." She met his gaze and her lips thinned. "The next morning, I woke up in a bed I didn't know, half naked. I thought that was possibly the worst moment of my life, but as you now know, it wasn't. Jake and Scott took that picture of me and shared it on the college discussion website with a message that read: A pretty piece from NYU. We destroyed her. Who wants her next?"

Rhys clenched his jaw, controlling the hot rage burning through him, and he watched every twitch of muscle on her face. She took another deep swallow, obviously shoving her sadness back to that place where she kept it to survive. "Can you tell me why you never reported them?" he asked gently.

She gave a small shrug, glancing down to her wringing hands. "Because I wasn't technically raped, so I thought the punishment wouldn't be severe. Ultimately, I just wanted to finish school, get the hell out of there, and move on."

He suspected she hadn't moved on at all, but it wasn't his place to make a remark on that. "You obviously wanted your own type of justice, since you went to great lengths to show them you were still a virgin."

Her response was immediate, her chin lifting in clear

defiance. "I wanted to show them that they didn't break me. That, yes, I was a virgin, and I was smart and strong enough to get close to them to show it. That, if I wanted, I could always get close to them. I wanted them to feel their control slip."

Shy, but brave. Strong, but hurting. This woman utterly fascinated him. "That's what this is about?"

She gave a firm nod. "This time, and every time from here on, I give my consent. My choice. My rules."

A raw truth lived in her eyes. Power too. Such remarkable power he had a hard time looking away from her. "What did you get out of the experience, then?" Everyone had their own reasons for coming to Phoenix. To leave the person they used to be at the door and come out someone different.

She took a moment to consider his question then answered, "In a month, I'm moving back to my family in Sacramento. I need to leave New York, leave all of the reminders here. I've lived in this sort of hell for the last year. I feel stuck in this pain because this dark cloud is always there, hanging over me, suffocating me. I refuse to be the person I am right now when I move. Last night, I left all my shit at your club's door. No more pain. No more thinking about those bastards. I'm officially moving on."

It all sounded logical, but Rhys knew most women usually led with emotions. "I think that all makes a lot of sense, but the question begs to be asked: did you not want to give your virginity to someone you love?"

"I can't love," she said, holding his stare.

"Can't or won't?"

"Can't," she repeated with a slight shrug. "I've tried to date. I can't get past the first date. And even on the first date, I have full-on panic attacks. I know it's hard to understand, but my virginity didn't mean what it used to mean to me. It's not special or sacred. It was a dark cloud over my life. And

I'm glad it's gone. That was *my* choice, *my* decision. And in the end, with the financial gift, I can move back home, buy a house, and have the life I should have had before two assholes decided to ruin everything."

Rhys listened to the trees rustle in the breeze, unable to take his eyes off her. He had seen people hurting before, and he could split them into two types. One hiding from their pain. The other dealing with it. Zoey was the latter, and he found her awareness refreshing. He'd been there once too. Hell, he owned Phoenix because it was part of his recovery after Katherine passed away. Her death was not easy; she fought death right to the end, and with her last breath, she screamed at the injustice of it all. A sound that haunted him ever since.

He'd opened Phoenix out of frustration and anger that Katherine's life was cut short, with so many hopes, dreams, and desires unfulfilled. Back then, he held back. After Katherine died, he stopped holding back from what he truly wanted. He'd stepped down as CEO of Harrington Finance, the company his family owned. He bought the cigar club as a playground to indulge his voyeuristic desires and to keep his emotions out of the game. Of course, with the frustration and anger over Katherine's death fading, he enjoyed what the club brought to others. Freedom and happiness. He found fulfillment in seeing others living authentically.

"So," Zoey said after a long, deep breath, drawing Rhys from his thoughts. "Are you upset with me for using your club for my own personal gains?"

He took a moment to examine her. She thought she was this hardened woman. That question proved her wrong. Pain hardened people. Rhys had seen that happen to Katherine, and she never recovered. Her cancer had created a hatred in Katherine that became all-consuming, and Rhys couldn't pull her out of that darkness. But Zoey wasn't hardened. She wouldn't care if he was upset if she was. "Upset, no, but I'd like to know how you managed all this. How you not only found out about the club, but also managed to get on the inside."

She shrugged and gave a sly smile. "A girl can never tell her secrets."

He gave that smile back. "To let this matter go, I need to understand how you breached my security. Save me the trouble of digging. You owe me that."

She watched him closely, obviously judging his character as a couple strode by, hand in hand. She must have liked what she saw on his face, because she hedged, "I didn't necessarily breach your security. My roommate Elise is a private investigator. For the last year, we've been keeping an eye on Jake's and Scott's texts and emails."

"In hopes they'd say something?"

"You know, I don't even really know what I was waiting for. It's like I knew to get my justice against them, I had to keep tabs on them."

"And then you learned they were members of my club?"

She gave a slow nod. "That's where my other roommate, Hazel, came in. She's a reporter. Good with research. Between my friends, we learned what we could, and then," she cringed, "Elise hacked your system in order to get the passcode to fill out the application."

Unbelievable. He stared at her, speechless.

She studied his face and winced. "I'm sorry. I know that's so wrong, but when I weighed my options, this gave me a way to leave all this hell behind me. Are you going to press charges?"

He snorted a laugh. "Press charges? No, Zoey, I'm impressed, actually, and considering offering your room-mates jobs." She'd found out the unfindable, or so he'd believed. He could only imagine Archer's irritation when he discovered the system he thought unfaultable was anything but.

Those thoughts vanished with her satisfied smile. A much better look on her than pain and tears. She looked like she was breathing easier now. For years, he'd tried his best to do right by others, to bring them happiness so people felt satisfied with their lives. So that no one felt like Katherine did. That when someone died, they knew they'd lived their life to the fullest. But there was something about Zoey, something he couldn't quite put his finger on. Something that told him not to walk away. Something that had him wanting more. "I have a proposition for you."

Her eyebrows rose atop twinkling eyes. "What sort of proposition?"

"Spend more time with me."

"Why?" She gasped.

He couldn't fight the slight chuckle that escaped him. "What Jake and Scott did to you that night has created revolving pain that you never deserved. But I'm here to tell you there is more to life than pain. Let me show you." Before she could think on it too much, he took her hand and rose, bringing her close against him until there wasn't any space between them. Her body against his felt oddly...*right.* Even with the dark night around them, he caught the flushing of her cheeks, the parting of her lips, begging for a kiss. "Here is my proposition: spend your final days in New York City with me. Let me show you how you should have been treated. How intimacy *should* be."

"Why would you want to do that for me?"

He hesitated then told her the truth. "Because the look on your face when you removed your mask haunts me. That pain is burned into my mind. Don't leave New York City with that pain. Let's erase it. Together."

She took a step back. "I'm fine."

He stepped forward. "Are you?"

"Yes—" She hesitated, and something shifted on her face, a coldness breaking into uncertainty. "Okay, maybe I'm not totally fine, but—"

"You're surviving, right?"

Her eyes searched his. "I guess you could say that."

He got that. He'd been there once too. Surviving watching Katherine die, and hating every second of not being able to save her. "When did 'just surviving' end up being good enough?" Oddly protective of her and determined to help her heart weather this storm, he added, "Last night, I took your virginity. You gave that to me willingly, and I appreciate the hell out of it, believe me. Now I'm asking for you to give me…*more*. Can you offer me that, too?"

"But why?"

For her. For him. For this connection between them that he couldn't quite figure out but couldn't let go of, either. "Ah, that's where you'll have to trust me. Think about it." He took a business card out of his wallet and offered it to her. "That's my personal cell number. Text me if you want what I'm offering."

She examined the card then lifted her heated gaze. "Which is what exactly?"

He lowered his mouth to hers until they were nearly touching. "To find that out, you'll have to say *yes.*"

And just as she reached for the kiss, he strode away. "Better get going. We don't want you to be too late."

Her soft curses had him grinning like a fool for the rest of the walk.

* * *

ONE-NIGHT STANDS WERE SUPPOSED to be emotionless and distant, but nothing about Rhys was cold. In fact, he'd been attentive and thoughtful last night when he took her virginity. He listened to every word she said on their walk like it mattered to him. Even as she strode next to him after their talk, his imposing height and muscular form, matched with his social status and wealth, should unnerve her, and yet, she felt more comfortable with him than almost anyone. Especially since the assault. But that little voice in her head that told her men were dangerous stopped her from immediately accepting his proposal, no matter how intriguing. She needed her friends to weigh in.

When Rhys stopped at the Devil's Café, a cocktail bar in the heart of Manhattan, Zoey spotted Elise and Hazel already sipping their fancy drinks, with Zoey's unopened bottle of wine waiting in front of the empty seat. A little pang hit her heart. Those martinis looked delicious, but she wouldn't dare drink anything not opened in front of her. Not anymore, probably never again.

"This is goodnight, then."

Rhys' warm, velvety voice lifted goosebumps across her arms. She met his eyes and felt an unexpected heat rush through her. Rhys was deliciously...*intense*. She'd never experienced the draw of a man. Against all her judgment and trust issues, she wanted to move closer. "It is goodnight. Thank you for walking me."

"I was very happy to," he nearly purred, closing the distance between them. He stood over her, this powerful presence of a man, looking at her with a smoldering gaze. "Goodbye, Zoey." Then his hand was cupping her cheek and his lips met hers, promptly taking Zoey somewhere other than the streets of Manhattan. God, the man knew how to kiss.

When he finally pulled back a long while later, she slid back into her body and reached for more. His throaty chuckle hit her like he'd stripped all her clothes off and entered her as he did last night. She snapped her eyes open to find a devilish grin on his face. "There is no expiration date on my offer," he told her before walking away.

She remembered how to breathe and gasped for air. Sudden loud voices and cars honking hit her. She blinked, following Rhys' long, steady gait until he faded off into the shadows.

Reminding herself how to walk again, she entered the cocktail bar and was greeted by the pop music and her two best friends gawking at her.

"What in the actual fuck?" Elise asked by way of greeting when Zoey reached the table.

Zoey slid onto the wooden chair. "I wish I could explain, but I don't even understand what's happening." She opened the wine bottle with the opener left for her and poured herself a gigantic glass.

Hazel's eyeballs were bulging out of her head. "That was Rhys Harrington."

Zoey took the largest sip she ever had, cringing against the dryness. "He was the guy," she said after she swallowed.

"The guy, guy?" Elise asked. "The one who took your virginity?"

Zoey nodded. "Yes, *that* guy."

"Jesus," Hazel breathed.

Zoey nodded again…and again… "If you think that's crazy, then wait 'til you hear this." She recapped what had happened since Archer picked her up at work until they just saw her kissing Rhys-fucking-Harrington. They both knew exactly who he was through the research they'd done on Phoenix.

When Zoey finished, Hazel gave her head a few shakes. "Yup, yup, that is crazy." She planted her hands flat on the table. "Okay, first, are you going to go to the cops with the evidence?"

She didn't even need to think about it. "A part of me knows I should come forward. Maybe they've done this before. Maybe they'll do it again. But the other part of me is terrified. I know what it feels like to have my whole world exposed and twisted. If I speak up, my life will be ripped apart. *Again.* And I would probably get blamed. I just don't feel strong enough for that right now. I want to focus on moving on."

Elise reached across the table. "You deserve to move on and be happy."

"Yes, you do." Hazel nodded firmly, taking Zoey's other hand.

"Thanks." Warmth flooded Zoey's chest as she squeezed their hands back. She never expected the friendship she had with Hazel and Elise. Leaving them would not be easy, and that stupid lump rose in her throat again.

Zoey washed it away with a long sip of her wine as Hazel asked, "Okay, so now, let's circle back to Rhys Harrington taking your virginity. Did you know it was him last night?"

"That's a gigantic no," Zoey responded, but then she hesitated, reassessed. "I mean, I guess I should have because of his eyes. He's got these incredibly smoky eyes, so powerful and intense. I've really never seen anything like them. But I didn't think about that until I saw him earlier."

"Yeah, yeah," said Elise, waving Zoey on.

"Hey, ladies." All eyes went to the cute thirty-something guy grinning at them. "Can I get you all a drink?"

"No," Elise said firmly, leaving no room to argue. She pointed back to the bar where his smiling friends were watching this show. "Go."

The guy's brows shot up. "Go?"

Elise dismissed him by looking away and focused back on Zoey intently. The guy stood, confused for a moment, but then slowly turned and walked away, facing his friends in defeat.

Zoey chuckled. Obviously, her story had Elise enthralled. She'd never seen her friend react so briskly.

Elise didn't miss a beat. "How about you tell us why Gorgeous Eyes just gave you the kiss of a lifetime outside?"

Because he's sweet? Because he feels obligated to help me now? "I think maybe it was to tempt me," Zoey admitted.

Hazel's eyes went wide as she nibbled on the end of her straw. "To tempt you to do what?"

"To want more of him."

The music blared through the speakers, the loud, excited voices spreading out in the room as Zoey glanced between her friends. A long moment passed then they all burst out laughing.

Zoey wheezed along with them, grabbing her belly. "Ow, ow, okay, stop."

Elise wiped the laughter tears from her eyes. "I can't help it. As if Rhys Harrington needs to tempt you. The man is fucking hot!"

"I know." Zoey breathed, leaning back in her seat. "This whole thing is absolutely ridiculous. I go from having no sex to having sex with one of the hottest men in New York City, who can have any woman he wants, but apparently, he wants more of me."

Hazel's smile died halfway through Zoey's statement. "I actually don't think that's weird at all. I mean you're entirely different than anyone he has probably met."

"She's not wrong," Elise agreed after a moment of consideration. "He deals with people who live a passionate lifestyle and who are rich. They aren't innocent dog-grooming virgins. Maybe he finds you refreshing."

Zoey thought that over and finally shrugged. "I actually think he finds my pain refreshing."

Hazel blinked. Then blinked again and frowned. "I don't even understand what that means."

"I don't really know how to explain it," Zoey countered, "but it's a feeling I get from him. Like he wants to…I don't know…take my pain away…" Elise grabbed her cell from the table and began typing as Zoey added, "In some weird way, I think he likes protecting women or bringing them happiness, or at least, that's what it seemed he was saying to me. He wants to show me a life I don't know exists, a life where a man doesn't hurt a woman."

"So, he's a fixer?" Hazel asked.

"Yeah, a fixer. That's a good way to put it," Zoey agreed. "And, seriously, do I really want to be someone's therapy project?"

Hazel gave a firm nod. "If that therapy includes hot sex with Rhys Harrington, then yes."

Zoey laughed, but stopped when Elise slid the cell phone across the table. "Who is this?" she asked, staring at a beautiful brunette.

"Katherine Rothschild," Elise said. "Rhys' late girlfriend."

Zoey looked up. "What happened to her?"

Elise took her cell back and began scrolling. "She had cervical cancer and lost her battle. She was only twenty-four years old."

"Wow, that's sad," Hazel said.

Zoey agreed with a nod. "Which is a red flag, right? I mean, this guy owns a sex club and obviously has baggage. Probably best I stay away." She couldn't ignore red flags anymore. Those flags kept her safe.

"Maybe," Elise said with a shrug. "Maybe not. I think, logically, anyone who has lost a loved one would do whatever they could to make sure the people around them were living their best life. If you ask me, I think it's kind of sweet that his current goal in life is to make others happy and satisfied."

"But he owns a sex club," Zoey reminded her.

Hazel said dryly, "Which is probably why he's such an incredible lay."

"Seriously?" Zoey gawked.

Hazel giggled. "Well, it's true, isn't it? You came home last night with stars in your eyes. That guy has got mad skills. Why not enjoy that for a while? You deserve all this and so much more. Hell, he wants to give you hot sex, and then you move. What could go wrong?"

"Everything," Zoey countered in haste. "Absolutely everything could go wrong." Because it had.

Elise gave her a soft, supportive look and reached across the table again. "The difference here being that this is your choice. Your say. Your rules. Maybe what he's offering is exactly what you need. Let him shake you out of your box, see the world with different eyes for a little bit then you can move back home, with the orgasmic glow that you deserve."

Zoey considered, sipping her wine, smelling the oaky hints. "Can it be that simple, though? That good?"

Hazel's eyes narrowed thoughtfully before she nodded. "If I can give my two cents, you're at a crossroad now. You faced the one thing that terrified you. The two men who assaulted you. Now fate has tossed you a chance at something different, something new. Do you want to be that same scared woman you said you wanted to shed? Or are you this new Zoey who is doing life her way, on her terms, no matter how impossible it seems?"

It all made sense. But… "It's really scary for me to let anyone in like that, even if this is sort of like an arrangement." Though a *new* little voice in her head reminded her that when Rhys was there, she seemed to let go easily. That maybe this wasn't so scary after all. And without a doubt, he'd stood up for her, protected her.

Elise lifted her glass to her mouth. Before she took a sip, she said, "Honey, life isn't fun if it isn't scary sometimes."

Zoey snorted. "Yeah, that's why I've lived very comfortably on the boring side of life lately."

Hazel grinned, smacking the table with her hand. "Well, now it's time to live on a different side, like Rhys Harrington's sexy-as-hell backside."

"It is a pretty spectacular backside," Zoey agreed with a laugh.

"So," Elise drawled, eyes dancing. "Does that mean you'll be seeing more of him?"

Zoey pointed to her wine and smiled. "I need at least two more of these before making that decision."

Elise reached for the bottle and filled up her glass. "There, now you can make the best decision of your life."

CHAPTER 6

"*L*ate night?" Rhys mused the next morning as Archer strode into the office on the main floor with dark circles under his eyes. After Rhys dropped off Zoey, he'd returned to the cigar club, where Archer waited for answers. Over a drink, Rhys gave them. He didn't need to come down hard on Archer's failure to keep the club safe. The guilt and frustration were etched into every line on Archer's exhausted face. Whatever weakness was in the system would get fixed and any threat handled. Of that, Rhys was certain.

"Very late night," Archer muttered, dropping down into his usual spot on the leather couch beneath the window, a file folder in his hand.

Rhys got up from behind his desk and took the wing-back chair across from Archer. The sun was trying to break through the clouds after the rain early this morning. This was the only time of the day when the club was quiet. The cigar bar didn't open until eleven o'clock, but morning meetings with Archer were part of Rhys' day-to-day.

"What's in the file?"

"It's—"

"Who pissed you off?" Hunt asked, gaze set on Archer, as he entered the office followed by Kieran, with coffees in hand.

Rhys grinned at his friends. Neither Hunt nor Kieran worked for him, but they were both there for one specific reason. To find out if they would be partaking in the show tonight. They were as much a part of the Phoenix family as Rhys and Archer. Rhys knew part of the success of his club was not just the stars, but the regulars who partook in the shows and knew how to fuck and give his members something glorious to look at. That passion made others want to watch. It was addictive, even to Rhys.

"Elise Fanning pissed me off," Archer said to Kieran.

Kieran offered Archer a coffee before taking a seat. "Should we know that name?"

"Maybe not, but I suspect you won't forget her."

"Consider me intrigued," said Kieran, leaning back in his seat and crossing his ankle over his knee. "Who is this mysterious Elise?"

"She's Zoey's roommate," Archer explained, taking the lid off his paper cup and sending steam rising. "She's also the private investigator who got past my security and hacked into Phoenix's system."

Hunt took a seat in the other wing-back chair and whistled. "I'm guessing that explains your mood."

Archer set his coffee down on the table in front of him and scrubbed his face. "I don't know how she fucking did that. All night, I've been on with my best hacker, and he can't see how she got in. She didn't leave a single fucking trace."

Rhys nodded his thanks to Kieran for the coffee and opened the lid to take a small sip, tasting the rich hazelnuts in the brew. He didn't want to suggest that perhaps Elise had a better hacker in her pocket, or she *was* that hacker, but...

"You should talk to her. If there is someone better out there, getting into places you thought were impenetrable, let's get them on our payroll."

Archer agreed with a nod. "I'd like to dig a bit deeper here to see what comes up. If that doesn't bring anything more to light, I'll get in contact with her."

"Good," said Rhys, trusting Archer to handle that. A security breach was inexcusable, but Archer would get to the bottom of it; Rhys didn't doubt that. "What have you found out so far?"

"That she's better at my job than I am," Archer mused.

Hunt chuckled. "Ah, so that's what is getting under your skin."

Archer's jaw set, and his eyebrow lifted in Hunt's direction. "Wouldn't it, yours?"

"Yes," Kieran answered for Hunt. "He'd already be at her house, knocking down her door, demanding to find out how she outsmarted him."

"Damn right, I would," Hunt said without remorse.

Rhys chuckled.

Archer wasn't amused. He snorted, shaking his head, and slid his gaze to Rhys, gesturing at the file. "Elise worked as a private investigator right out of high school, mentoring under Luke Hicks. Three years ago, she went out on her own."

"Who's Luke Hicks?" Hunt asked.

"The best PI in New York City."

"Ah," Kieran said. "Explains why she's so good, then."

"Yeah, it does," Archer hedged, the corners of his eyes tightening. "Beyond that, nothing I discovered links Elise to any current members. A past member used her once to gather evidence against her cheating husband, but it doesn't look like she uncovered anything about the club in that investigation."

Rhys pondered this, knowing they had to look at this from every angle to ensure the Phoenix members were safe. They paid him to keep their sexual kinks out of the public eye. The breach couldn't happen again. "Do you believe the story Zoey told me?"

Archer considered it and gave a quick nod. "Her other roommate, Hazel Rose, is a reporter, so that is another truth to her story. Everything she said lines up."

Kieran asked, "Does Hazel have any connections to any members, current or past?"

"Not that I could find," Archer reported, a hard frown marring his face. "From the outside, I'm leaning toward believing them. They're a group of determined women that used their skill set to fight against an injustice."

"Sexy," Hunt said.

All heads nodded in agreement. Even Rhys found himself enamored by the wit and strength of these women. What they'd pulled off was impressive, considering Archer's background in security. But Rhys already knew there was nothing to fear more than a scorned woman. He believed Zoey.

His cell phone beeped on his desk, indicating a text message. He set his coffee down, rose, grabbed his cell, and swiped the screen. He couldn't hide his grin at the single word from Zoey.

Yes.

"Now, that looks like good news," Kieran called at whatever showed on Rhys' face.

"Depends," he said, returning to his seat and reaching for his coffee again. Of Archer, he asked, "How much of a risk is it if I invite Zoey back to the club tonight?"

Archer's gaze held Rhys' for a beat, his mouth twitching. "When do we ever invite women who are not members back?"

Rhys returned the hard stare. "That's not the question I asked."

Hunt broke out into laughter. "I've got to get a look at this one. She must be something special if she's got Rhys breaking rules."

Rhys didn't look Hunt's way. He didn't have the words to explain what had caught him up in Zoey. He only knew he wanted more of those sweet, innocent eyes looking up at him. That lush body, bending to his will.

Archer cocked his head and said to Rhys, "A higher risk now that she's already been dishonest. How can we trust what she's telling us as the truth?"

Rhys inclined his head at that statement. He never took risks. It kept his members safe. But when it came to Zoey, he couldn't help himself. "Call it a gut feeling," Rhys offered.

"The risk is still there, nonetheless," Archer countered firmly. "While I tend to agree that whatever Zoey wanted to do, whatever point she wanted to make, she did that the other night. As your head of security, I would caution you to proceed slowly. Zoey is not a member, which means the rules do not apply to her. She could out our members."

Rhys sat back. He knew Zoey wouldn't say a word about Phoenix if he asked her not to. "All right. Caution noted." He turned his attention back on to his phone and fired off a text to Zoey: GO TO THE CAFÉ ROUGE ON E 79TH STREET. 8 PM. GIVE THEM YOUR NAME. He took another sip of his coffee as he shoved his cell into his pocket and addressed the group again. "Anything else to discuss today?"

"Nothing here to report," Hunt said.

"All good here." Kieran rose. "What's the show tonight?"

Archer stood and grinned at Hunt. "Hampton"—a famous actor—"wants a bondage, blow-job show with your favorite."

"Aw, I do love that gorgeous brunette," said Hunt, heat flaring in his eyes over the twenty-six-year-old brunette he knew nothing about. Neither Rhys nor Archer would break confidentiality, even though Hunt was as close as a brother to them. Hunt had set his sights on Lottie Harlow the night of her first show. He'd been lusting after the well-known regular at Phoenix who many members specifically requested. Lottie had originally gained membership through another member who she was engaged to, and her fiancé paid for her membership. Her fiancé enjoyed watching her with other men. When they broke up, Rhys intervened. Lottie could barely pay rent, let alone the steep membership fee, so she asked to become a permanent star. Rhys had never let a star come back more than once, but since Lottie was a previous member, and since other members had requested her participation in their shows, he agreed. Now, because of her popularity, she made an income higher than most doctors, and the work was definitely far more satisfying. To Rhys, Hunt added, "When are you ever going to throw me a bone and get me in a show with her?"

"When you stop wagging your tongue at her," Rhys told him.

Hunt barked a laugh. "Never going to happen. Damn, that woman haunts my dreams."

"Exactly. You're too invested," Rhys called over his shoulder on his way to his desk. He took a seat, looking Kieran's way. "You interested?"

"Fuck, yeah." Kieran slapped Hunt's back and gave him a shit-eating grin. "Don't worry, Hunt, she'll take real good care of me."

"Lucky bastard," Hunt breathed, envy seeping into his gaze.

Before they all left, Rhys said, "Show up tonight. All of you."

All eyes turned back to him, but it was Hunt who asked, "Why? Planning something special?"

Rhys grinned and knew that for them to understand his intent for the evening, he only needed to say, "I could use some extra hands."

* * *

ZOEY SPENT the day cleaning the loft and doing a week's worth of laundry to keep herself from thinking about returning to Manhattan tonight. But the time came, and Zoey left Brooklyn behind and made her way into the city. Though, this time, she noticed a slight change on the subway ride. Her excitement to see Rhys again stole some of the cold fear away. An idea that bewildered her, until all thoughts vanished as she arrived at Café Rouge. She couldn't stop gawking at the quaint space. She wasn't sure what she'd expected to find after Rhys' invitation, but a coffee shop didn't scream *sexy*. A few people sat at the booths along the left-hand side while one person worked behind the counter. Not seeing anything else to guide her on what she was meant to do next, she approached the barrister.

"Hi," the thirty-something blond woman said. "What can I get for you?"

"I'm not quite sure," Zoey answered. "I'm Zoey Parker."

"Ah, Zoey, I've been expecting you. Please come with me," the woman replied with what Zoey took to be a pleasant smile. "I've got what you need just in the back."

Zoey hesitantly followed, not wanting to look back to catch anyone's eye. She stayed close to the woman into the back storage room. Boxes of coffee lined the one wall, and there was a small kitchen, where some baked goods were currently sending scents of warm apples and cinnamon the air.

"I know it doesn't look like much," the woman said, "but

we've got some cool hiding spots." She pulled open a shelf with glass canisters, revealing an old set of stairs.

Zoey leaned forward and glanced down, peering into a place where any sane person wouldn't go. "What is it?" Zoey asked.

"The tunnels from Prohibition," the woman explained. "They used them to secretly get alcohol into the cigar club. When Rhys bought the bar, he also bought all the businesses where the tunnels ended."

"That must have been expensive."

The woman gave a grin that told Zoey how stupid her statement was. "The Harrington family is old money, honey. I imagine it didn't break the bank."

A flush crept over Zoey, but she clamped down against it, refusing to let the old her run the show. All of this was out of her league, and she totally wasn't this bold and brave woman, but after all she'd been through, she deserved this thrill. She *needed* this thrill. "So, I just go down there, then?"

"Yup. Just walk to the end of the tunnel. Security will greet you there."

"Okay, thank you." Zoey began the climb down the ladder.

Right before the woman shut the shelf, she gave a wide smile. "Enjoy yourself tonight, honey."

"Thanks. That's the plan." Zoey returned the smile, continuing her climb down as the light above her vanished.

When she reached the bottom of the ladder, she saw a long, straight tunnel made of old stone, and if she closed her eyes, she could swear she caught the scents of the oak barrels that must have been hidden down here through Prohibition. Brightly lit sconces lined the walls as she made her way down the tunnel, her high heels clicking against the cobblestone floor. She rounded one bend at the very end and then came to a stop outside a wrought-iron door. She knocked once, and the loud unclicking of a lock echoed in the underground tunnel then the heavy door slowly opened, revealing a small room, not much bigger than a walk-in closet.

"Good evening, Zoey," a security guard with kind eyes said, like they were already friends. "Rhys has been expecting you. Please come in."

"Thank you." She stepped through the door, feeling like all of this was impossible. That, any minute now, she was going to wake up and realize this had all been some wild, incredible dream.

The security guard locked the door behind her and moved to the small desk, where a telephone and computer rested. He had the phone to his ear a moment later. "Zoey has arrived. Yes. All right. Very well."

He returned the phone to the receiver right as another door to Zoey's left opened and a gorgeous brunette wearing a tight black dress walked in. "Zoey, hi. I'm Lottie."

"Hi," Zoey said, finding it near impossible to stop herself from gawking at the woman.

"My eyes, right?" Lottie asked with a lopsided smile.

"I'm sorry for staring," Zoey said in a hurry. "They're just the most beautiful color I've ever seen. Are they—"

"Amethyst," Lottie finished. "Yeah, and yes, before you ask, they're one-hundred-percent natural." She gestured for Zoey to follow. "Come on, we don't want to be late. Everyone gets grumpy when that happens."

Zoey wasn't exactly sure what she was going to be late for, but she gave the security guard a goodbye wave and stepped through the doorway. "Where are we going?"

Lottie linked her arm with Zoey's. "To shop."

Two doors down the hallway, Zoey understood what Lottie meant. They entered a room the size of a boutique, only this room was full of high-class lingerie. Wall to wall, there was every type of fabric, from leather to lace, in the entire color wheel. "Wow," Zoey breathed.

"I know, right?" Lottie shut the door behind them then gestured out. "Go on, pick whatever you like for the night."

"Seriously?"

Lottie nodded. "Free lingerie is part of Phoenix's membership."

"But I'm not a member," Zoey gently reminded her.

"You're Rhys' guest," Lottie countered. "That's one and the same."

"Where does he get all this?"

"It all comes from a shop here in Manhattan. The owner, Adalyn, is a longtime Phoenix member."

Zoey's brows shot up. "I thought this club was a private one. Masks. No names. No identity. That type of thing."

Lottie shrugged. "Adalyn uses her name on the regular, probably because Phoenix members are rich. She wants the clients." Lottie went quiet and tilted her head, giving Zoey a long once-over and approached the racks with the green lingerie. She picked out a sexy, strappy, dark-teal set. "If you ask me, go for this. You'll look amazing in this color."

"It's gorgeous. Thank you."

Lottie handed Zoey the piece. "The changing room is right over there." She gestured to a small fitting room off to the side. "The heels you have on will look great."

Zoey moved to the changing room, closed the curtain, and began undressing, feeling the heat rising to her cheeks. "Do you work here?"

"Work, not exactly," Lottie said with a smile in her voice. "Play, yes, and I just so happen to make some good cash from that."

"It's a good way to make money," Zoey mused, slipping out of her dress and hanging it on the hook on the wall.

"You can say that again."

Zoey removed her panties, replacing them with the new ones. After she finished with the bra, she slid back into her heels and then opened the curtain, finding Lottie standing there, wearing an intricate metal mask and dark-red lingerie that did amazing things to her figure. Dangling from her fingers was a gorgeous gold-and-black metal cat masquerade mask.

"This was Rhys' only request for you tonight," Lottie said with a sly smile. "Here, turn around. I'll help you get into it."

Zoey turned, only then catching her appearance in the mirror. When Lottie settled the mask in place, she stared at her reflection. Who was this woman? Zoey barely recognized the strength in her eyes, the confidence, the beauty. But then she remembered she wasn't this woman at all. Her arms instinctively wrapped around herself, her gaze lowering to the floor.

"Oh, hell no, girl," Lottie said, tucking a finger under Zoey's chin until she was looking at herself in the mirror again. As she uncrossed Zoey's arms, she said, "The most powerful man in this club requested you be here tonight. Rhys never does that." She stepped behind Zoey and said, dead serious, "Ever, Zoey. So, don't be shy or meek. He could have anyone, and he wants you. Just *you*. Own that shit!"

"I'm not used to this," Zoey admitted, rubbing at the back of her neck. "I'm just not this woman."

Lottie grinned. "You are now." Her gaze flicked to the clock on the wall. "Right on time. Perfect. Let's get this show started." She strode off, and Zoey forced her feet to move and did her best to hide her nerves. They headed down another hallway, and Lottie stopped at a door. "Enjoy the show, Zoey. It was great to meet you."

"Nice to meet you too. Thanks for the pep talk," Zoey said.

Lottie gave a quick smile and entered the room.

Only she didn't stop to mingle. Lottie headed straight for a gorgeous black-haired man who wore a mask that, to Zoey, looked slightly demonic and yet sexy all at once. Though it might have been that he was bound to the stone wall, with leather straps covering his arms, that increased the appeal. One look at Lottie heading his way, and the man went from soft to hard in a heartbeat.

Damn, to have that power. What must that feel like? It occurred to Zoey that she wanted to find out. She was aware of other people around her, but she couldn't look away as Lottie kissed the man like she'd been starved of him. After she took her fill, leaving the man's breath rough, Lottie slowly lowered to her knees, and Zoey felt herself grow damp between her thighs as Lottie took the man's cock into her mouth and slowly began teasing him.

With every move of her mouth, every tremble and moan the man gave, Zoey felt pleasure coursing through her, building more and more heat between her legs. She could tell he wanted to look down, to watch this talented woman giving him what looked like a mind-blowing blow job, but the binds refused him. As the minutes dragged on, Zoey became lost in the erotic energy pulsating in the room, the crowd silently watching, admiring, enjoying. Until she felt a hard body step in behind her. She inhaled in surprise but caught Rhys' aroma, something that was close to the woodsy oak barrel scent she'd noticed in the tunnels, with a little bit of added spice.

"You like watching her pleasuring him?" he asked, pressing his rock-hard erection against her bottom.

She melted against him, shivering at Rhys' breath on her neck. Suddenly, she needed what he'd promised. "Wouldn't everyone?"

"No, Zoey, not everyone likes to be watched or to watch." He nipped at her neck. His voice lowering to a seductive purr. "But you do, and so do I." Her eyes rolled back into her head as his hand reached out to stroke her belly. Any timidness left, vanished under that powerful touch. "Tell me, what about this do you like most?"

She angled her head, giving him better access to devour her neck. "All of it."

"The bondage?"

"Yes."

His hand inched its way lower. "Is that what you'd like, Zoey, to be tied up for my own personal use? For my pleasure?"

"Yes," she whispered, needing him, wanting *more.*

Her breath hitched when his finger sneaked into the top of her panties. "Does it turn you on how she's sucking his cock, drawing him deep into her mouth? Making him shudder and lose control?"

"Oh, yes." She gasped as his fingers stroked over her sensitive clit, taking her far away from there. "I like watching her control him like that."

Rhys' low chuckle brushed against her neck, causing goosebumps to rise along her skin. A deep groan escaped him when his fingers touched her drenched heat. "Would you like to own me like that, Zoey. To control me? To do whatever you want to me?"

"Yes." She moaned, wiggling her hips into the pleasure.

He nipped at her neck at the same moment he began stroking her clit faster, harder. "Another night, I will be yours. Tonight, I'd like to play. Will you let me?"

Her legs began trembling as pleasure cascaded into her. "Yes. Please."

"Whatever I want?"

Another moan broke free. "Yes." Her eyes slowly opened to the bound man's groans growing rougher. Lottie moved fast now, bobbing on his cock. And Rhys' finger began moving faster and harder on her clit. Zoey felt in rhythm with the man being brought to climax, and she was *right* there.

Every muscle in the man's body flexed, an impressive sight to behold. He struggled against the binds as he growled, bucking into the pleasure. The same euphoria overtook Zoey. Wave after wave of hot sensation stormed across her, leaving her a trembling mess of satisfaction.

She stayed in the warm, blissful place until reality returned as the clapping started. Again, she reopened her eyes, discovering that, while most of the crowd was watching the show, the people closest to her and Rhys were clapping in their direction.

Still behind her, Rhys placed a soft kiss on her shoulder. "Go back down the hallway you just came. Find the door that this key opens." He placed a vintage skeleton key in her hand. "I'll be waiting for you there."

She felt a cold void as his strength left her, and she turned, only to find a door shutting behind him.

When she faced the crowd again, she felt all the watchful eyes on her, obviously curious over this new woman who had Rhys' attention. But she couldn't find it in herself to be shy, or even ashamed that she'd orgasmed in front of them all. She glanced down to the skeleton key in her hand with trembling legs, wanting only one thing.

More.

CHAPTER 7

A little adventure never hurt anyone. Which was precisely why Rhys didn't tell Zoey the location of the room where he waited for her. He wanted anticipation to build, and with every door she tried to unlock, adrenaline would spike in her, creating the intensity he wanted her to feel tonight.

Rhys sensed the others in the room experiencing the same eagerness, and he smiled. The erotic nature of his lifestyle fueled his happiness. Back when Katherine was alive, he'd only begun to taste the heightened senses that came from exploring eroticism. Back then, he held back. Katherine's death had taught him not to.

When the lock finally turned with a loud *click*, Rhys cleared his thoughts, watching the door slowly creak open. His back was pressed against the far wall, arms folded over his chest, while Zoey froze in the doorway. The cat mask he'd personally chosen for her tonight looked far more beautiful than he could have imagined. Her body exuded purity and innocence, and yet her eyes behind that mask were heated and greedy. And both of those contradictions had his cock swiftly hardening to steel.

Zoey looked from left to right, absorbing the view, and obviously taking stock of Hunt and Archer in the room, along with two female members, who were setting the stage for Rhys tonight and already naked. Both men wore condoms.

Hunt glanced Rhys' way and received a quick nod. Hunt sent Zoey a wicked smile before he moved behind his lover for the night, Aimee, and began caressing her breasts. Archer was on the other side of Hunt, already kissing Bianca, putting on the sensual show Rhys asked them to. They all knew the plan tonight. The stage Rhys had set was planned right down to the hundreds of candles casting a warm glow throughout the open space. The walls were old stone, and the only furniture in the room was an old kneeling bench lined with red velvet.

Rhys stayed put, allowing the atmosphere to further excite Zoey. Those pretty cheeks darkened, her lips falling open as she drew in heavy breaths. His cock twitched as she watched the others engage in foreplay. They were beginning to heat up, the intensity building.

Zoey blinked, finally releasing the door and letting it shut behind her.

She went to take a step forward, when Rhys called, "Stop." He noted the widening of her eyes at the same time she teetered on her sexy heels. He'd never used that tone, low and unyielding, and it dawned on her that this game belonged to him. "Undress for me."

Those cheeks of hers went ruby-red. She looked at Hunt then at Archer, and their lovers, who stopped their activities to watch her.

Rhys smiled, knowing full well she would soak her panties before they dropped to the floor. He stayed quiet, giving her the time to decide. Though it did not surprise him when she reached back and unhooked her bra. She was far braver than she gave herself credit for. And he hoped by the time she left New York City, she would realize it. Her bra dropped to the floor a second later, revealing her puckered, light-colored nipples. Considering the room was warm, Rhys grinned in delight of how aroused she was. She was a dream come true, turned on by eroticism, eager to please and explore. When she began removing her panties, Rhys caught the slight glistening of her arousal on the inside of her thigh before she stepped out of the cloth. Rhys licked his lips and scanned her, naked, exposed, and ready, from head to toe, a sight of womanly perfection. He'd seen many naked bodies. None like hers. None that made him want to bring her in close and not let go.

He caught the tightening of her hands into fists, the stress no doubt nearly suffocating her. To ease her nerves, he glanced at the group. "Tell our guest what's on your mind right now."

Hunt swung his arm around Aimee and grinned sensually. "I'm thinking it's a damn shame that tonight will end without me inside you."

Archer didn't miss a beat. "You're a lovely treat for us all," he murmured, squeezing his partner's bottom.

Bianca added, "He took the words right out of my mouth."

Aimee stopped from licking her way up Hunt's chest and grinned sensually at Zoey. "I'd like a taste of all that sweetness you exude." To Rhys, she added, "Can I have her?"

Zoey's mouth parted with clear surprise, those wide eyes most definitely a treat for all.

But sharing had never been Rhys' style. "No, you may not."

"Pity," Aimee drawled then returned her tongue to Hunt's chest.

Rhys smiled at her and then addressed the group, "But you can have each other. Make Zoey ready for me."

He saw Zoey's slight shudder at the same moment he sensed his friends take things up a level, pressing their ladies against the walls to offer pleasure and take it too. Rhys could only watch Zoey, noting how the compliments had lifted Zoey's shoulders a little bit more. Which was why he'd asked the question. To show her, to prove to her, that she wasn't only there as a participant, but that she was the damn star of the show. That this night was for her. And secretly, for him too.

Her breath grew raspier as she watched the lust unfold. Rhys let it play out. Out of the corner of his eye, he noted Hunt hook Aimee's leg on his arm. Heard Aimee's gasp, followed by Hunt's grunt as he roughly entered her. More importantly, Rhys saw Zoey's heightened reaction, squeezing her legs together tightly.

"Give yourself what you need," he told her. Zoey's gaze flicked to his, and he added, "Pleasure yourself."

He expected her to do as he told her, but what he hadn't expected was how remarkably beautiful she looked when one hand found her nipple and the other slid between her thighs. Her chest rose and fell with heavy breaths as she stroked herself, pleasure washing across her expression.

His cock twitched, and he fought against his desire to take her. Around him, Rhys sensed the others turn to watch her, this innocent beauty that should not have the sensual nature she exuded, and yet it was there, captivating the room. When she began stroking her clit faster, her eyes focused on something, Rhys followed her gaze. Hunt had started pounding Aimee from behind, his hands tight on her hips. Archer had his lover up against the wall, thrusting in long, slow strokes. All of which wasn't by chance. Rhys wanted to watch Zoey and learn. Her tells. Her wants. Her desires. And she was revealing everything. She kept her gaze locked on Hunt, her cheeks bright red now as her hand between her legs sped up.

Rhys grinned at Zoey. *Ah, you like that, sweet one?*

Her legs trembled before her movements became rough. She squeezed her nipple, eyes closing, gasping in big breaths.

When she hung on the edge of her climax, Rhys called, "Stop."

Her hands stopped moving, but those gorgeous legs still shook. Rhys' cock ached at her responsiveness, at her natural ability to fall into this sensual lifestyle.

"Go to the bench. Bend over it. Spread your legs."

Her gaze flicked to the one-way mirror running the full length of two walls. She was smart, wondering if members were behind that glass, and obviously now aware that when she bent over, they'd all see her, most intimately. From what Rhys had seen of her reactions so far, he suspected she'd like that. He didn't know how many members were watching this show, but he knew word spread like wildfire when he partook in an unplanned personal show. He tended to draw crowds.

Zoey held his gaze like she'd done it a thousand times, the side of her mouth curving slightly, and something seeped in the air between them. Something most unexpected. A feeling like he was her anchor. That as long as he kept his eye contact with her, she would be okay. He would be okay. And together, they could do anything. When she finally bent over the bench and spread her legs wide, Rhys didn't hesitate. He liked the way her eyes heated, knowing others saw her in a way no one had before, but he wanted to feel her. To be in the one place only he had been before. To feel her break apart around him again.

Slaps of skin, deep moans, and the musky scent of sex filled Rhys' senses as he dropped his pants and sheathed himself in the condom he'd brought with him. Nothing beat the intense and needy way she looked at him. He doubted anything could compare.

When he stepped in behind her, knowing without a doubt that the members watching had all moved to the other side of the wall to get a better view, he slid his fingernails along her back. She arched into him, and he chuckled, hearing lust vibrating in the sound. He leaned down and said just to her, "I want to fuck the living shit out of you."

"Then, do it."

A challenge. There was a part of him that knew he needed to go slow, be gentle. But that part had left with her consent. He kicked her legs open wider until her feet rested just at the sides of the kneeling bench. This particular piece of furniture had been handpicked by Rhys tonight to bring her up to his height. He thrust his hand in her hair until he had her angled where he wanted her. Then he entered her in one swift stroke, unsurprised at how easily he did so. She was primed and ready, and she rose up on her tiptoes, letting out a rough sound of surprise as he gripped her hip.

He went nearly cross-eyed at the tightness strangling his cock. Allowing himself a moment to enjoy himself, he tipped his head back and relished in the beauty of her body. But when he glanced back down, he caught sight of his fist in her hair, her eagerness, waiting for him, and any control he had fled him. He lowered his chest to her back and growled in her ear, "Tell me to be gentle."

"No," she breathed.

Fire licked his veins as he closed his fist tighter and did what they both wanted: he pounded her sweet heat, unrelenting. Each thrust came harder and faster than the one before it. Until there was no one else in this room but them.

Nothing else there but the pleasure that their bodies created. Nothing but this insane need she brought out in him, this hunger, this chemistry.

With every moan she offered, every shudder she gave, he felt her take something. Something that she could never give back. Something that he didn't want back. And when she screamed her pleasure and broke apart around him, he followed her. He came in a loud roar, bucking and jerking until he emptied himself inside her, until all he sensed was the magic brimming in the air between them. The gap between fantasy and reality coming to a head.

Drenched in sweat, he leaned over her again, and he kissed her neck, patiently waiting for her to return from her climax. Her sex milked him, drawing out all that he had and seemingly wanting more. He knew then this wasn't the end. That he would break more rules for Zoey. She had him ready to throw out the whole damn rule book.

CHAPTER 8

A day later, sitting in the grooming room between clients, Zoey couldn't stop thinking about her night with Rhys. Hell, she'd thought about it all day and night yesterday and even had to take out her vibrator to settle herself before she could get to sleep. Her belly still flipped and flopped at the erotic adventure she'd been on, and she swore she could feel every one of Rhys' touches brushing across her flesh. While all of this was like some amazing dream she never wanted to wake up from, the little voice in her head reminded her that, while it felt good to be this brave, sensual woman, she couldn't forget people weren't always who they said they were. Even though she was having incredible sex with Rhys and he appeared to want to protect her, she really didn't know him at all.

A dog's loud bark snapped her eyes open. She stared at the quote another groomer had put on the wall: "A DOG IS THE ONLY THING ON EARTH THAT LOVES YOU MORE THAN HE LOVES HIMSELF." JOSH BILLINGS.

Sometimes, Zoey loved dogs more than people. She looked above the quote to the clock and cursed. She was five minutes late for her next appointment. In a rush, she hurried out to the waiting room, where a pup was whining.

"Hilary?" she called.

The woman with the honey-colored hair sitting in the corner stood. "Hi. Yeah, that's me."

"Come on this way." Zoey waved her forward and led the way back to her grooming room. "I'm sorry I was a couple minutes late."

"Oh, that's no problem at all."

Zoey smiled in thanks and shut the door behind them. She immediately turned her focus onto the caramel-colored Labradoodle and squatted next to the dog, giving her head a scratch. "You must be Daisy. Aren't you just the cutest?" She touched around the dog's neck and ears and belly. "I feel a few mats, but those shouldn't be a problem. How short do you like her? Or do you have any pictures you want me to look at to go off of?"

At the deafening silence, Zoey looked up to meet Hilary's gaze, and that's when she knew one thing for certain. Hilary was not here to get her dog groomed. Zoey didn't know if it was the sadness in Hilary's eyes or the paleness of her face, but all her internal alarms began blaring. And yet...*and yet,* she couldn't move, because Zoey recognized that look on an intimate level. She'd seen it in the mirror when looking at herself for the last year.

"It happened to me, too," Hilary said softly.

Zoey swallowed. *Hard.* "I don't know what you're talking about."

"You do," Hilary replied, her voice shaking, eyes pleading. "I didn't know how to do this, how to approach you and not scare you. But what Jake did to you, he did the same to me, too."

Zoey wanted to move, to run, to do anything, but she remained motionless, frozen by the fear racing through her.

"I...I...don't know what you're talking about. I don't know a Jake. I need you to leave. Right now." Needing desperately to get away, she shot up and flew back against the grooming table.

"No, please, no." Hilary reached out, grabbing Zoey's arm. "I don't want to scare you. We have to fight against him. We can be strong together."

Rapid thoughts rushed through Zoey's head. *How does she know about Jake? How did she know I confronted him and Scott? How?* The room spun a little as the blood slowly drained from Zoey's face, making her legs wobbly. "I don't want to fight against anyone. Whatever you're thinking, you're wrong. You need to go."

Hilary's grip tightened. "You need to fight. *We* need to fight."

The woman was obviously not taking no for an answer, and Zoey ripped her arm away, moving farther away into the room, near the window. "No, I'm sorry. I can't help you." The thought of her life being exposed again, ruined in ways she could never imagine, crippled her. "I can't do this."

"They won't believe me," Hilary implored, tears welling in her eyes. "If it's just me who comes forward, it won't be enough. It's Jake's word against mine. You know him. He's rich and powerful. He'll get this buried. They'll destroy me."

"Exactly," Zoey shot back. "No one will believe us. Jake already ruined my life once. I can't let that happen again."

"But we can try," Hilary said, stepping forward. "We can fight."

Zoey's lips parted, *yes* nearly leaving her mouth. Her heart roared to fight against the injustice that had been done to her. But at the image of her life being front-page news, bringing down a big gun on Wall Street, had her stomach roiling. Heat blasted across her, bile rising to her throat. She rushed to the trash can in the corner of the room and emptied the contents of her lunch. "I'm sorry," she breathed when she could speak again. "I can't do this...can't help you... I just...I can't go through that again."

Hilary blinked, tears flooding her cheeks. "I understand, I do, but he can't be allowed to get away with this. If we don't stop him, this never goes away. It'll always be there, haunting us." A nameless, dark emotion crossed her face. "Haunting me." She blinked as more tears fell down her face then reached into her purse. "This is my card. Please, if you change your mind, call me. No matter the time. I'll answer." She grabbed the dog's leash and strode out of the room.

Zoey shot forward toward her purse on the counter, her heart ready to jump out of her chest. She had her cell in her shaky hands a second later.

Elise answered on the first ring. "Hey, babeolious, what's up?"

"I don't even know how to explain what just happened," Zoey managed.

Elise paused. Then, "Tell me everything."

Zoey took a few deep breaths and knelt down, getting her bearings. She finally answered, "A woman just came into the clinic. She said she's been assaulted by Jake too."

"Wait...*what*?" Rustling came through the phone line. No doubt Elise was moving to her laptop in her bedroom. "Seriously?"

"Yes," Zoey breathed.

"Did she mention Scott?"

"No," Zoey said, pressing her hot hand onto the cool floor, grounding herself like her therapist had once said to do whenever things felt too out of control. The technique had gotten Zoey through those last two months of college. "Just Jake. Elise, tell me I shouldn't be freaked out right now."

"Don't be freaked out." She paused as clicking on her keyboard sounded through the line. "I'm sure everything is fine. Of course Jake likely had other victims. I just want to figure out how she knows you. Did she tell you her name?"

Zoey glanced at the card she'd dropped to the floor. "Hilary. No last name. She gave me a handwritten card with her name and a phone number on it."

"I'm on it." The phone line went dead.

"Is everything okay?"

Zoey glanced up, discovering Betty, the receptionist, in the doorway. Her dark, concerned eyes told Zoey she needed to lie through her teeth. "Yes. Yes. I'm sorry. Everything's fine. The lady ended up wanting to take more time to decide the type of cut she wanted me to give her dog before we proceed."

Betty's brows shot up. "She seemed upset when she left."

"I don't think so," Zoey said and gathered herself to give her a smile. "She said she'll be back."

"Oh, okay." Betty returned the smile, obviously believing the lie. "All done for the day, then?"

"Sure am. Any plans for the night?"

Betty grinned. "I've got a date with Netflix. See you tomorrow."

"Bye," Zoey said, still stuck on the ground, her legs nowhere to be found.

Betty gave a final wave and strode away.

Zoey leaned back against the grooming table and released the breath she hadn't realized she was holding. The room swam a little. She shut her eyes and breathed past the panic creeping up her throat. She was done with lies. Having just told one made her feel like crawling out of her skin.

Her cell phone beeped in her hand. She expected Elise, but that wasn't who texted her.

THE GUYS AND I ARE GOING FOR DINNER TONIGHT AT SKYLINE. INTERESTED IN JOINING US?

She stared at the message from Rhys, feeling like the

world was determined to keep messing with her. Was this a date? Okay, no, his friends were going. Did that make her one of his friends? Friends with benefits, maybe?

All the logical parts in Zoey's brain fired off a hard response of "no". Wasn't it better to keep things strictly to Phoenix? But her head was spinning, her heart all types of confused. Both Elise and Hazel were working tonight, which meant she'd be left alone with her thoughts. Feeling a step away from falling back into that dark place she'd just crawled out of, she fired off her response. WHAT TIME?

7:00 PM. SEE YOU THEN.

Zoey pressed her cell phone against her chest and exhaled. One breath after another, after another, after another. A few more weeks was all she had to get through. Then she could leave this city and her pain behind. Until then, she had Rhys…and his ability to help her forget everything.

* * *

STARS BLANKETED the sky later that night when Rhys answered his phone. "Hello, Mother." He sat atop New York City's hottest dinner spot, Skyline, a rooftop restaurant. Lights from the high-rises were gleaming as far as the eye could see.

"Rhys, my dear, how are you?" his mother, Alice Harrington, asked, her voice soft yet lacking the warmth Rhys had heard from other mothers.

"Things are good here," Rhys replied, one arm stretched across the bench seating. "I take it you've been sent the quarterly report?" Earlier today, Harrington Finance delivered the report he knew his father had been waiting on.

"We did receive it, yes," Alice said. "But that's not the only reason why I'm calling."

Yeah, right.

Rhys kept the thought to himself as Alice replied, "But since we are talking about it, your father was quite pleased with this quarter."

"I'm sure he was." Profit for the Harrington fortune was up ten percent for this last quarter. Rhys' personal finances were up by twenty percent, something he kept to himself. Rhys took the Harrington fortune under his wing when he'd stepped into his father's role at Harrington Finance when his father retired, but that stress became tiresome. Especially after Katherine's death. Wealth had its advantages, but it could not buy happiness, and it certainly didn't buy his. Now Rhys' cousin William was CEO of Harrington Finance, and while Rhys was still involved in the decision making, he had taken a big step back to his father's fierce displeasure. Now, alongside being CEO of the cigar club, he also invested his money as a silent partner in up-and-coming companies, hedge funds, new drugs and research for cancer, and real estate. Rhys had questioned his choice of walking away from his family's powerful company, but the move had been a smart one. He now had full financial independence from his family's wealth and zero of the stress. "Anything I need to hear on my end?" he asked, moving the conversation along.

"Nothing more than your father was pleased," Alice said. "How's the cigar club?"

"Profitable." Rhys' relationship with his parents was that of responsibility, business, and privilege. He didn't fault them for it. He'd been raised by nannies and sent to boarding school. But he respected his parents. They were both good people, who gave back often to charities, and not only for the tax break. But the truth was, and always had been, his friends were his family.

"And a wife?" Alice inquired. "Any news on that front?"

"Nothing to report," Rhys said in a dry voice.

She laughed softly. "I'll take that as a no. Don't take too long, Rhys. You do not want to be an old bachelor. You know what your father will say about that."

Rhys didn't comment. He never did. Some people, he owed explanations to, but his parents were not among them. As he saw Archer, Hunt, and Kieran approaching the table, he said, "I need to run, but before I do, tell me how the traveling is going?"

"Europe is beautiful, very magical," Alice explained with an unusual sense of wonder to her voice. "We've been enjoying ourselves."

"Glad to hear it. We'll talk soon. Goodbye."

"Goodbye, Rhys."

He ended the call right as Archer took a seat to his right and asked, "How's your mom doing?"

A soft laugh escaped Rhys, and he shook his head. His expression must have been stiff. Phone calls with his parents always brought Rhys back to that life on a very tight rope. When his parents retired and began traveling, the rope had stopped strangling him. "She's well."

Hunt took a seat next to Archer and gave a slow whistle. "Curiouser and curiouser."

Rhys didn't even have to look to know Zoey strode through the restaurant's doors. He could see it written all over his friends' faces. But Rhys had already decided to break rules for Zoey. There was no going back, and even if Rhys was questioning his decisions, he wasn't about to stop where life was taking him.

Archer set a firm gaze on him. "You better know what you're doing."

The reprimand was expected. The rules had always been clear. No mixing personal and Phoenix business. "She's moving in a couple weeks," Rhys said, rising from his seat. "The risk is minimal."

Kieran snorted a laugh. "Keep trying to convince yourself of that, buddy."

Rhys ignored the reproach. Right now, his intent was to show Zoey that there was so much more to life than what had been handed to her. She'd told him she couldn't even go for dinner with a man without having a panic attack. He hoped that this dinner was a step in the right direction. His friends rose to greet Zoey when she sidled up to the table. "Hello, Zoey," Rhys said, leaning in to kiss her cheek.

She smiled at his friends then set those beautiful eyes on him. "Hi," she said, just to him.

At that sweetness aimed his way, he knew he walked a dangerous line. He liked the warmth of her. A little too much. But as long as he stayed behind that emotional line, the risk was minimal for them both. When he backed away, he said, "Zoey, this is Hunt and Kieran, very good friends of mine, and you already know Archer."

"Hi, yeah, I do. Nice to meet the rest of you," she said with the innocent smile he was growing fond of. Until her eyes narrowed a little and awareness came to them, and Rhys fought his laughter. Obviously, she'd recognized Kieran from Lottie's show and Hunt and Archer from their private show the other night. She quickly looked away, pink-cheeked, then turned to Rhys, clearly needing direction.

He took her hand, bringing her in next to him. Once she sat, he glanced at Kieran and gave a quick nod. Kieran immediately caught on and said, "We got a call out to a lightning strike today." His friend had always been able to deliver a fantastic icebreaker. Which was exactly why he'd asked his friends here tonight. He hoped Zoey would be at ease, see that this wasn't a date, and that she was simply joining him and his friends for dinner.

When Zoey visibly relaxed next to him, Rhys explained, "Kieran's a firefighter."

"Really?" Zoey said. "That must be exciting work."

"Sometimes," Kieran said with a slight shrug. The darkness behind his eyes said not all aspects of the job were good.

Rhys caught the eye of the waiter and gave a flick of his chin. The waiter came over and opened a bottle of white wine, as Rhys had instructed, pouring Zoey a glass from the just-opened bottled. He'd already noticed how she wouldn't drink at the club, always requesting a can of something unopened.

He asked Kieran, "Was anyone hurt?"

"Thank you," Zoey said to the waiter when he finished pouring.

Kieran shook his head in clear amazement. "Everyone survived, but how, is anyone's guess. The lightning hit a tree and traveled through the roots, striking a man who was sitting out in a chair on his lawn. That same tree smashed into the house, crushing the living room. Luckily, the wife had just left the room."

"Someone was watching out for them," Hunt breathed.

"Definitely," Kieran agreed.

"The man was wearing rubber shoes, right?" All eyes turned to Zoey. "That's what saved his life. The shoes?"

Kieran nodded. "Had he been barefoot, he wouldn't have survived."

"Are you ready to order?"

Rhys only then noticed the waiter had returned to their table. He glanced Zoey's way. "Surf and turf okay for you?"

"Sounds amazing," she said with bright eyes.

Rhys smiled at her and said to the waiter, "Then, surf and turf it is for the table."

Thirty minutes later, Rhys leaned back against the bench, sure he couldn't eat another bite. The platter in the center of the table was empty, the plates wiped clean. However, the more he took stock of Zoey tonight, the more something seemed off about her. She stayed quiet through most of the dinner, her shoulders curled slightly.

As Archer and Hunt talked about the other night's Mixed Martial Arts fight, Rhys slid a hand on Zoey's knee. She jumped at the contact, but he kept his hand there. Truthfully, he didn't know the inner workings of her mind just yet, but he didn't take her as the type to be so withdrawn. "Is this too much for you tonight?"

"No, no." She exhaled slowly and gave a small smile. "This is actually really, really nice. It feels good to be out with other people than Hazel and Elise and not losing my shit completely." She nibbled her lip, obviously weighing the option of telling him more. Delight spread through him when she decided to share. "A woman brought her dog in for a grooming today, but things got weird," she said.

"Weird, how?" Rhys asked.

She glanced around, obviously wanting to keep the conversation private, then she leaned forward and said quietly, "She told me Jake assaulted her."

A fork clanged on a plate. Zoey jumped. Rhys didn't even have to look to know she now had everyone's attention at the table. He saw the panic in her expression and rushed to explain. "As I'm sure you've already figured out, these men are like brothers to me. We share everything, which includes any developments at the club. They knew your story before I truly knew you. Nothing you say and nothing they have already learned will ever leave this table. You can trust them, Zoey."

She looked each man over one by one then gave a slow nod. "Okay."

Sounding much like the detective he was, Hunt asked in a steady voice, "Do you know the woman?"

Zoey shrugged. "I have no idea who she is. I know her name is Hilary. Elise has been looking into her, but she had to work tonight, and things are moving slowly on learning more about this woman." Her worried gaze connected with Rhys'. "I can't figure out how she knew what happened."

He took her hand and squeezed tight, noting the tremble of her fingers. "We'll find out, believe me. But the question begs asking, did she know you confronted Scott and Jake at the club? Or is the timing just suspicious?" To Archer, he added, "Thoughts?"

Archer leaned his elbows on the table, gaze focused on Zoey. "It could be as simple as this woman went to the same university as you. She could have heard what happened directly. And that the timing of all this is a coincidence."

Zoey shrugged. "That's what Elise is looking into now."

At that, Archer frowned. To Rhys, he still looked mildly annoyed at the mention of Elise, but he added, "More likely, she's a member of the club and put two and two together when she saw Scott and Jake leave." His gaze returned to Zoey, his voice softening. "Did she say what she wanted from you?"

"She wanted me to come forward," Zoey answered. "To make Jake pay for what he did. To get justice."

Archer's jaw clenched, a telling sign he didn't like what Zoey had said. "And you told her that's not an option?"

She gave a slow nod. "I just…I—"

Hunt interjected, "Do not need to explain yourself or your choices to anyone."

A look of pure relief washed over her face. "Thanks for that." She sighed heavily and added, "All I want to do is put this behind me."

Rhys had never been prouder of his group of friends. He hadn't had a woman in his life for so long, he forgot what it felt like to not only protect her himself, but have his chosen family protect her too.

"You deserve to do that, too," Archer countered. His head

cocked as his stare became probing. "What did she do when you told her you wouldn't come forward?"

"She gave me her card with her phone number and left," Zoey said, voice thickening.

Rhys squeezed her thigh, the only comfort he could give.

"Did you enjoy the surf and turf?" the waiter asked, sidling up to their table once more.

Rhys nodded. "Dinner was excellent. Compliments to the chef."

"I'll tell him you said so, sir," the waiter said with a proud smile. "Any dessert to cap off the night?"

Rhys looked to Zoey. She held her stomach. "I couldn't possibly eat another bite," she said.

Everyone at the table shook their head, so Rhys responded, "No, thank you. We'll just finish our drinks."

"Excellent," the waiter said. "Enjoy them and the rest of your evening."

When he wandered off to likely print off the bill, Rhys asked Archer, "Did any other victims come up in your investigation?"

Archer gave a slow shake of his head. "I didn't dig that deep." *There will be more,* his expression declared.

Rhys was determined to make sure Zoey didn't feel pressured. Her choices were hers. Only hers. Always hers. "Did you feel threatened by her?" he asked, rubbing her thigh, not liking the tense set of her muscles beneath his hand.

"Not at all," she replied after a moment of consideration. "I was shocked by her appearance, but not threatened. It felt like she wanted an ally."

Rhys reached for her hand again, encompassing her fingers in his hold. The guilt, the pain, the loss of control in her gaze shattered him. He said to Archer, "Find out who she was. How all this is connected."

"Elise is already on it," Zoey said.

Again, Archer's eyes narrowed, but his grin declared it was game on. He rose and was heading for the door a moment later.

Kieran chuckled. "Oh, that roommate of yours is getting under his skin."

Zoey cringed. "I'm sorry."

"Don't be," Rhys interjected, reaching for the bottle of wine to top up Zoey's glass. "Archer lives for this shit."

"*H*e brought you out with his friends," Hazel said the next morning while Zoey slipped into a white-lace summer dress in the changing room of a boutique in downtown Brooklyn. The little shop belonged to a young designer who, as far as Zoey was concerned, should have been showing her clothes on the runway. She zipped it up halfway as Hazel added, "That's a statement, girl."

"A statement declaring what?" Zoey asked in all serious-ness. "He knows I'm moving. Besides, we both know he wanted to help me get over all my hang-ups. I told him I couldn't even date a guy without having a panic attack."

"Yeah, well, I don't really think Rhys is the type of guy to let anything stop him from getting what he wants."

Zoey agreed wholeheartedly. Even as she played it cool, she stared at herself in the mirror, seeing a new kind of happiness on her face. A dangerous kind of happiness because Rhys wasn't supposed to be making her feel this way. Better, yes. Healthier, yes. Sexier, yes. Emotionally connected, hell no. She released a breath, noting a new kind of warmth in her chest. Last night, she'd felt protected, not only by Rhys, but by his friends. Being honest and open with people other than Hazel and Elise felt...*good.* Hell, trusting more than her roommates and her parents felt incredible. She grabbed the curtain and peeked out at Hazel. "Tell me that continuing to see him is a huge mistake. That I should stop whatever is happening right now. That I am actually in way over my head and this is going to end up with me devastated and even more broken."

Hazel gave a lopsided grin. "Well, you're not broken. You're awesome. And Rhys is rich, gorgeous, and obviously has a soft spot for you. Why on earth would I tell you to stay away from him?"

"You wouldn't," Zoey hedged. She'd be *insane* to stay away.

"You're right. I wouldn't," Hazel agreed with a firm nod. "Now get back out here, and let me see that dress on you."

Zoey hurried to do just that, all the while questioning where exactly life was taking her now. She'd decided to move. Start over. And yet...*Rhys.* Everything felt different than it had when she walked through Phoenix's door. She felt different. Before, she'd felt like she wanted to run away. Now she wasn't sure why she was running. She loved her friends, her job, her life in Brooklyn, and she was beginning to love this new erotic life she'd found. She was even beginning to not hate Manhattan. Sure, she missed home too, but she could visit often. That lump in her throat rose up again, but she forcibly swallowed it back as she whisked the curtain open.

"Oh, you must get that," Hazel said with big eyes from the other side of the store.

"Isn't it gorgeous?" Zoey shifted from side to side, studying the white-lace summer dress that fit her like it was made for her. "But it's also expensive."

"Oh, please." Hazel stopped to glance back as she shifted

through the skirts hanging on the rack. "Do I need to remind you that you can afford it now?"

"I guess," Zoey hedged, running her hands over the lacy fabric, wondering what Rhys would think of this dress. Would he like it? Would he want to take it off her immediately? Would he think of something totally erotic to do with the dress? "Okay, you're right, I never do anything like this," she finally said. "It's just so pretty. I must have it!"

"Hell yeah, you do," Hazel said, going back to the skirts.

By the time they were done shopping, Zoey'd only bought the dress. Hazel bought a long maxi skirt and a crop top that showed off her midriff. Before long, they returned to the subway and headed back home.

When they finally made it back to the loft, shopping bags in their hands, Hazel whistled. "Well, that's certainly a nice view to come home too."

"You're not kidding," Zoey agreed, embracing the butterflies filling her belly as she spotted Rhys leaned against his black sports car in front of the loft, scrolling through his phone. Her heart flipped over a few times, threatening to melt in a puddle. His head slowly lifted, eyes connected with hers, and the corners of his mouth curved slightly. Heat flooded her from head to toe, all pooling into a needy throb between her thighs. Oh, the power this man had over her body was unreal.

"Hello," Hazel said by way of greeting. "I'm Hazel."

"It's nice to meet you, Hazel," Rhys said, without any of the heat Zoey was used to hearing in his voice. He offered his hand. "Rhys Harrington."

Hazel returned the handshake. "Mm-hmm, good to meet you." To Zoey, she grinned. "I'll see you inside."

"Okay." Zoey turned to Rhys after Hazel slipped into the loft. "Hi."

"Hey." There was that heat, nearly sending her soaring backwards like an erotic punch to her gut. "How was your day?"

"Good," she answered, shifting on her feet, but stopping immediately when she felt her damp panties. To get her mind and her body out of the gutter, she asked, "Have you heard anything from Archer about that woman?"

"He's still on it."

"Elise, too."

The sun beamed down on Rhys, revealing auburn highlights in his jet-black hair that she'd never noticed before. He gave a nod and a warm smile. "Then, hopefully, we will have answers soon." His gaze flicked to the shopping bag in her hand. "Looks like we were both shopping today." He turned back to his car, reached into the open window, and pulled out a small bag.

Zoey's heart still hadn't recovered from the last flip, and promptly did a little dance now. "You bought me a gift?"

"For tonight, if you'll oblige me."

"You didn't need to do that," she said, heat rising to her cheeks.

"I know I didn't have to, but I wanted too." He offered the bag. "Open it later."

"Okay," she said, wondering why he didn't want her to open it now. Considering people were walking up and down the street, she figured maybe it was something naughty in nature. "Thank you for thinking of me."

"You're welcome." Then he leaned in and winked. "Though I have totally selfish reasons for buying you what's in the bag."

"Now I'm intrigued." She grinned.

"As you should be." He tucked his hands into his pockets, looking like some model plucked out of a magazine ad. "So, for tonight, I'm hosting a party at a property I own. I wondered if you and your friends would like to come."

Her mind went straight back to the gutter, but she immediately chided herself. Last night, they had done something so simply normal, eating out at a restaurant. "I don't think anyone has plans, so I'll definitely ask them."

"Excellent." He slipped his hands from his pockets to take her in his arms. "I'll send a car."

It was dangerous how easily she molded herself to him. "Do you need me to bring anything for the party? Food? Or anything."

"Just yourself." He dropped his chin and gave her a long moment to stare into his gorgeous, smoky eyes before his lips met hers. His kiss was full of promise of a night to look forward to. When he leaned away, his grin turned naughty. "And don't forget what's in that bag."

"I won't. Promise," she said, stepping out of his arms.

"Good. I'll see you later."

He opened his car door, and she waved. "Bye."

She forced herself to stay put and watched him drive off. She'd never met anyone like Rhys. He seemed so in tune with her emotional state, always doing whatever he could to reassure her. To help her move past what had happened. Doing sweet things for her. It made her aware she was doing absolutely nothing for him. When his car faded off in the distance, she decided that needed to change.

When she hurried inside, she found Elise on the loveseat, her legs dangling off the side while she ate popcorn. "Okay, I have to know what is in that bag."

Zoey laughed and asked, "Did Rhys knock earlier?"

"Yup," Elise said. "And he had that bag in his hand. I told him to come inside to wait, but he said he didn't want to interrupt my soap opera."

Hazel snickered. "Probably saved himself the torture."

"Yup, probably." Elise tossed a kernel into her mouth. "Actually, wait before you get to the gift. Let me tell you what I've learned about Miss Surprise-You-At-Work."

Zoey shut the door behind her and locked it before addressing Elise again. "Lay it on me."

"Her name is Hilary Du Pont, but she didn't go to school with you. Her family is rich, like stupid rich. Which, of course, leads me to believe she's a Phoenix member, but annoyingly, they've upped their security."

Hazel rolled her eyes. "I wonder why that is." She headed into the kitchen.

Elise grinned at the retreating Hazel. "It's nothing to worry about. Just makes me stretch my brain a little, that's all. I'll find out what I need to and will let you know."

"Please don't get into trouble," Zoey said in all seriousness. "Rhys has his security looking into it too."

Elise smiled, all teeth. "Oh, then, let the race begin." She had always been competitive in nature. At Zoey's heavy sigh, Elise laughed loudly. "Don't you worry. I won't get myself or you in trouble. I can handle Rhys' security. But enough about annoying security men. What did Rhys get you?"

Before Zoey could find out, Hazel returned with three wineglasses and handed them out. "What did Rhys say to you?" she asked, not having heard Elise's question.

"He actually invited us all to a party he's throwing tonight," Zoey said, sliding out of her sandals. "Do you want to go?"

Elise and Hazel exchanged a look and then said in unison, "Yes."

Zoey fought her laughter, waggling her eyebrows. "Didn't even have to think about that one, huh?"

"Not one bit," Hazel said, taking the seat next to Elise on the couch. "But what kind of party is this?"

"I suspect it's a PG-rated one," Zoey replied.

"Still fun," Hazel said. "I bet it's all fancy and stuff."

"Yeah, yeah, good stuff." Elise waved Zoey on then shoved more popcorn into her mouth. "Okay, *now* can we see what he bought you?"

Zoey set both bags down on the coffee table, plus her wineglass, then reached into the smaller one. Her fingers touched delicate lace before she pulled out a stunning black-lace bra. The type of that cost money. Expensive lace that had never touched her body before. "Holy, wow," was all she managed to get out before she caught more lace in the bag. She lifted out the matching panties, noticing the heaviness of them. "What…the…" She touched the front, feeling more to the material. "There's something in them."

Hazel took the panties, studied them, and a second later, her cheeks burned bright. "They're, you know, vibrating ones."

"What?" Zoey asked with a laugh.

Elise snatched them next, examining them this way and that. "I bought similar ones for fun once. I mean, not nice like this, and I suspect mine probably don't work as good, but they're vibrating panties that come with a remote control."

Hazel leaned forward, peeking inside the bag. "Is the remote in the bag?"

Zoey shifted through the paper. "No." She turned around, hoping she didn't lose anything. "I didn't see a remote. Did it fall out?"

"Yeah, into Rhys' hand." Zoey turned back to catch Elise's shit-eating grin, as her friend added, "And here you thought this party was going to be PG-rated."

* * *

THE HARRINGTON LAKE house had been in Rhys' family for three generations, sitting on Long Island's North Shore. The five-bedroom stone colonial house stood slightly atop a hill, which faced out to the water. Behind the house were manicured gardens designed to impress at parties. Three smaller cottages were spread out on the three plus acres of forested land. The property had been bought and used for business, though Rhys had many parties and spent a lot of time at the lake house during his teenage years. Now he held quarterly parties there to schmooze the right people, to keep his business connections tight, but he also invited Phoenix members to the party. Tonight, they were all in attendance, enjoying cocktails and live music beneath the canopy of stars and twinkling string lights. However, Rhys' focus had stayed with Zoey since she arrived. From the other side of the bar, Rhys couldn't fight his smile. He had yet to talk with her, but for the last twenty minutes, he'd been tormenting her with the vibrating panties through the remote control in his pocket, something she'd hid well from her friends. He couldn't take his eyes off every little wiggle of her hips, every moment she froze under the force of the pleasure, and the way her gaze searched him out.

When she turned again, looking for him, he decided to end both of their suffering. He turned off the vibrator that had been set to the lowest speed, and approached from behind her. "Ladies," he called. Zoey turned first, her friends' gazes following. He took Zoey in, every spectacular inch of her in the fitted white sundress. He wondered if this was what she'd purchased earlier today. He liked this look on her. A little innocent, definitely not overdone, and yet, she stood out as the most beautiful woman here tonight. She didn't have diamonds on her neck or wrist; she didn't need them. She sparkled without anything added. "Are you enjoying yourselves?" he asked them.

Zoey gave him a lopsided grin. "How couldn't we?"

Now closer to her, he caught the heat in her eyes, the pretty color in her cheeks. He laughed easily, something he didn't do often enough. She was in his arms a moment later, and he pressed a soft kiss to her lips, not particularly caring what kind of statement that made to anyone watching. "I'm glad tonight is hitting you in all the right places."

She laughed with him, but as he released her, a hand presented itself in front of him.

"Hi. Since we didn't get formal introductions at the house, I'm Elise."

He shook her hand. "It's nice to meet you, Elise." All three women were beautiful in their own way. Each unique and different than the women Rhys knew. No fake nails or fake eyelashes. Their dresses weren't designer, their hair not smoothed to perfection. He liked that about them. "I hope you're enjoying the party."

"It's incredible," Hazel answered with twinkling eyes. "I have never seen anything so beautiful as this—oh, look, champagne. I'll grab us some." She beelined for the waiter striding away from her with the tray holding the champagne flutes.

Zoey gave a soft laugh and an easy shrug. "Hazel gets easily distracted, sorry about that."

"Nothing to be sorry for," he said, honestly. He found all of them refreshing, but most of all Zoey, the woman making him break all his rules. "These parties can be a bit distracting. They're always showy." He turned to Elise and smiled. "I'll introduce you around later. This party is full of lawyers and politicians who always need a good private investigator in their pocket."

"I'd appreciate that. Thanks," Elise replied with sincere gratitude.

Just then, off Zoey's shoulder, Rhys caught Archer

approaching, and he chuckled. He'd seen his friend pissed before, but nothing quite like this. Archer's gaze was fixed on the woman they were well acquainted with now, but he grabbed two champagne flutes as he walked by.

Elise was saying something to Zoey that Rhys couldn't catch, but she went dead silent as Archer closed in. Her gaze scanned him from head to toe before her chin lifted and shoulders squared. Ah, so she knew exactly who Archer was, and by the slight curve of his mouth, Archer knew this too.

Eyes locked on her, Archer offered her the champagne glass. "Hello, Elise."

She gave a polite smile. "Hello, Archer. Thanks, but I don't take drinks from strangers."

Archer gave that smile back. "Let's not play games, shall we? We both know we're not strangers. You probably know more about me than I know about myself."

Her smile now showed teeth. "I could say the same to you."

Archer winked. "You probably could."

Zoey looked between her friend and Archer and gave a tight laugh, taking the champagne glass from Archer. "Thanks. I'd love a drink. This champagne looks yummy." She set it down on the table next to her.

Rhys shoved his hands in his pockets, chuckling at the tension pinging between Archer and Elise.

Something Hazel immediately noticed when she returned. She handed a champagne flute to Elise and asked, "What's wrong with you?"

Elise took a long sip, keeping her stare on Archer then smiled at Hazel. "Oh, there's just this annoying bug, buzzing around me, that I want to squash."

Rhys barked a laugh, unable to help it, not surprised one bit when he looked at Archer to find him grinning too. Elise was just the type of woman Archer liked. Strong, beautiful, but more importantly, a challenge.

"I really hate bugs," said Hazel, obviously unaware *who* the bug was. She sipped her champagne and let out a long sigh. "Beautiful night. Gorgeous party. Seriously, can this night get any better?"

"It can," Rhys said then offered Zoey his hand. "Let's go get you a drink."

"I've—"

"Leave that one," he interjected, knowing she'd never drink it, and understanding why. "Indulge me."

Zoey looked at her friends.

Elise waved her off, still in a fierce stare down with Archer. "We're fine."

Zoey's expression declared she didn't believe her friend. "No squishing bugs tonight, all right?"

"Can't promise that," Elise said, smiling at Archer. It wasn't a sweet smile.

"When did Zoey start caring about bugs so much?" Hazel asked Elise as Rhys took Zoey's hand and led her away.

"Don't worry," Rhys said to Zoey, tucking her arm in his. "Archer won't let her squish him."

Zoey asked softly, "He's pissed, eh?"

"That's probably putting it lightly. Archer is not used to someone getting by him, but I'd be willing to bet he's more intrigued than angry. He likely wants to get into her head."

"He'll need a key that no one has found yet to get inside that head."

If anyone could unlock a strong mind, it was Archer. He had the skill set, confidence, and patience of a saint. The man gained trust like Rhys had never seen, and he was owed that too. When they reached the bar, he said to the waiting bartender, "An unopened bottle of your best."

The bartender responded without question, dropping a

new bottle of champagne in front of Rhys, along with two glasses. Within minutes, Rhys had popped the cork, poured the glasses, and offered one to Zoey before adding to the bartender, "Whenever Ms. Parker would like a drink tonight, open a new bottle for her and pour the drink in front of her."

"Yes, sir," the bartender said then strode off to the next customer.

"You didn't have to do that," Zoey said, color rising to her cheeks.

"Yes, I did," Rhys said, leaning an elbow against the bar. "You deserve to enjoy a couple fine drinks as much as everyone else here."

She rolled her eyes. "Yeah, but those are my issues—"

Rhys had his arms around her, pulling her close. "Issues that are the result of trauma. You're not asking; I'm offering." He lifted his glass, wanting to show her that real men earned trust. "To a fun night."

She smiled softly, a new warmth in her gaze that made his chest expand, and clanged her glass with his. "To a fun night."

After she took a sip, he placed his glass back on the bar and drew her close again. "I'd like you to stay a little later after your friends leave tonight. I can drive you back to Brooklyn later."

"Oh," she said, wide-eyed. "So, you don't just plan on teasing me all night?"

"Never," he said, licking his lips when she licked hers. Damn, that mouth tempted him. Her innocence seeped into the air around him, tasting sweet and eager. "Ask them to leave at midnight, all right?"

"Okay," she said. "Am I in for a good surprise tonight, then?"

He lowered his hand from the small of her back to her bottom, pressing her against his erection. "A surprise? Most definitely." He dropped a soft, teasing kiss against her lips. "Midnight, Zoey, that's when our game will begin."

He leaned away and grinned a slightly dark smile when he caught the arousal in her expression. To move things along in the right direction for their night ahead, he turned away and chuckled to himself at her loud gasp when he set the vibrator to full speed.

CHAPTER 10

Shortly after midnight when the party ended and all the voices grew quiet, Zoey felt the energy shift in the air. Elise and Hazel had gone home, and so had half of the people in attendance. Zoey had said goodbye to her friends in the circular driveway as they hopped in the chauffeured car Rhys had arranged for the night. When she strode back toward the house, a security guard met her there. One she'd seen working at Phoenix before. He gave her a gentle smile and handed her a black metal butterfly mask. "Rhys requested you wear this tonight." He gestured down the lit pathway that led into the forest. "Follow it until it forks then go right."

Zoey glanced down the long stone path and smiled at him. "Thanks." Her stomach danced with nerves as she tied on her mask and followed the cobblestone path, but halfway down, she stopped short. Erotic moans filled the air, all blending together like a beautiful song.

"Zoey."

The low vibration of Rhys' voice hummed nearby. She

glanced back, finding him striding toward her, wearing only his black dress slacks, a gold mask on his face. His gorgeous body glistened with the soft hue coming from the gaslit lanterns. Every muscle flexed and moved with his long strides. He looked like a warrior that belonged in another century, ready to defend and protect against any threat. When he got close, he turned on the vibrator again, and a strangled moan broke from her throat, her knees weakening.

"You don't play fair," she said when he reached her. She'd never been so sensitive before. Maybe that was his intent.

"I never said I would play fair," he murmured, taking her hand and leading her forward, continuing around the bend of the pathway.

The night was a perfect mix of warm and dry, and when they broke free from the forest and entered a clearing, Zoey couldn't stop her surprised gasp. Not because of the light buzz against her clit, sending shock waves of pleasure through her, but in the middle of the clearing was a large round cushion a few feet off the ground. On it, dozens of men and women were engaging in every type of sexual act Zoey knew of, and some she didn't. The more she watched, the more she didn't know where some people began and some ended. It became impossible to absorb it all. Men were having sex with men in all stages of foreplay. Women were teasing each other while they rode the men beneath them. Masks covered identities, but naked bodies were being cherished. Sex being explored and indulged in, without any insecurities in sight. It occurred to Zoey that this was freedom. The act of simply enjoying what feels good without judgment.

She felt the sensual energy brush across her, the need consuming her. Before she could decide where to look, a man knelt in front of her, his big, hard cock greedily available.

"I'm at your service," he said to her. "Tell me what you'd like."

She stared down at the muscular man, who rested his hands on his thighs, awaiting her command. It was clear that whatever she wanted—any fantasy she ever dreamed up— she could have from this strong man.

"He wants to pleasure you," Rhys said from beside her, with no waver to his voice. "The choice is yours."

She became lost in Rhys' smoky eyes. The choice was completely hers. He would respect whatever she wanted, allow whatever would make her happy. But as she looked deeper into his molten eyes, a truth she couldn't ignore appeared. This wasn't just sex between them. It wasn't only about the eroticism, the game. Because if it were, she'd gladly accept this man's offer to experience something new, some- thing different. But she didn't want the man who offered her pleasure. And for all Rhys had done for her, all the kindness and strength and everything in between, she wanted him to know it. "I don't want him," she said, hearing the emotion touching her voice. "I want you, Rhys. Only you."

Something flared in his eyes. Something possessively hot and addictively sweet as she moved around the man kneeling at her feet. With hot moans of pleasure fluttering through the air, she settled in front of Rhys. He dipped his chin, his hands loose at his side as she reached for his belt and unbuttoned his pants. As she slid them down over his sculpted ass, she purposely ran her hands over him, and she relished the way his jaw muscles tightened.

She kept her eyes on him and slowly lowered to her knees next to the man, who rose and headed off elsewhere. Rhys stroked the side of her cheek, staring at her the way a wolf stares at its next meal. "I want you," she told him, reaching for his mighty cock. He was thick and hard as steel as she stroked him. She was no expert at giving a blow job, but she'd watched a sensual blow job porno on the Internet and studied every detail, learning ways to pleasure him like he'd pleasured her.

When she tickled her tongue around the tip's rim, she felt Rhys' hard shudder under her tongue. She wanted him to feel her appreciation, her trust, her gratitude for the woman she knew she was becoming in the short time she'd known him. The way he was mending all the shattered parts of her heart with little regard to what he needed. And with every swirl of her tongue, obvious desperation and need filled him, showing how much he needed to be touched too. Not out of sexual need, but from a deeper connection.

She kept her eyes on him like she'd seen the woman do in the video last night, while she sucked on each testicle then slowly dragged her tongue up the length of his shaft. Sometimes, she tickled, other times, she licked harder. She didn't need a manual to see when the teasing became enough and Rhys demanded more. His hot gaze told her as much. Not wanting to deny him what he was due, she closed her eyes and turned her full attention onto his cock. Heat flooded her when he thrust his hands into her hair and growled, a low, unforgettable masculine sound. He began pumping his hips, taking pleasure in her mouth, and she rejoiced at being the reason he felt so good.

Then his legs were trembling, his fingers tightening in her hair. She felt the seconds when he pulled back, like he wanted to ask permission. She grabbed two fistful of his ass and sucked her lips around the base of his cock. At that, Rhys' rough groan brushed across her, overtaking all the other moans coming from the orgy. Her mouth soon filled with his semen, and she swallowed quickly, loving the way he jerked against her, losing himself in the pleasure she gave to him.

When he finally released the tight grip on her hair and she looked up at him, his head was tipped back, his chest heaving, sweat glistening off his incredibly toned body.

She kissed his thigh and said up at him, "Whatever you want tonight, I am yours, Rhys."

He dropped his chin and his brows came together, an unfamiliar emotion reaching his eyes. Breathless, he gently stroked her cheek with his thumb for a moment, a beat passing between them. The next second, she was in his arms and he held onto her bottom as he walked them down another path, far away from the sex in the forest.

When the pathway stopped at a stone cabin, he moved them inside and set her down on the bear rug in front of the fireplace, into a kneeling position. The space consisted of a king-size poster bed. But she couldn't look away from the raw emotion on his face. He cupped her chin and held her gaze. "Explain this change in you."

She blinked at the seriousness of his voice. "What change?"

He leaned down, bringing his gaze down to her eye level. "You are looking at me like I can have your soul if I want it. Why?"

Tonight, all along, the plan had been to pleasure him like he'd pleasured her. Now, with those smoky eyes holding her captive, the truth seemed right there, ready for her to grab it. "Because you deserve the same kindness you give."

Obviously seeing the things she wasn't saying, he leaned in farther and asked, "Why?"

Emotion crept up into her throat. "Because you're a good man."

His fingers tightened on her chin. "Why, Zoey?"

The words fell easily. "Because I feel safe with you."

His voice turned rough, unhinged. "Why?"

For a year, she'd been caged in. So afraid to speak her truth, but not now. Not with him. "Because I trust you." She rose and cupped his face, moving closer until there was no space between them. "Because I have never felt like this with anyone, and I don't want to fight this. I'm sick of fighting the things I feel. Sick of refusing to believe good things can happen. I want you, Rhys. Not the fantasy. I want the man behind the mask."

His jaw muscles clenched once as she reached back and unlaced his gold mask. She let it fall from her fingers to the ground with a *clang.* Following her lead, he reached back and removed hers. Then his lips met hers, and this kiss was different. Everything about him was different. Rhys was a man who wore many masks, but he was her favorite without one. He kissed her with a hunger she couldn't catch up with. He kissed with meaning, with passion. But alongside all that, his kiss bled with pain. Loneliness. Neediness. Vulnerability. And those were things she understood.

Realizing she could give him exactly what he needed too, she quickly caught up with his intensity and kissed him back, climbing up his body until he had her in his arms, and he laid her out on the bed in the middle of the cabin. The bare tip of his cock touched her drenched folds. His kiss turned more urgent, his request loud even though he didn't say a word. Phoenix rules were clear: all participants had to provide monthly medical records showing negative STI and AIDS tests, plus all women were required to be on birth control. She trusted him, and in those tests, as she shifted her hips, taking him inside her. His rough groan brushed against her ear, and she shuddered with the same euphoria.

He rocked into her slowly, intimately, his eyes holding hers with every thrust. She explored his body with her hands, feeling all the muscles and grooves that made up this man. Soon, she felt joined, not only physically but emotionally, every shift of his hips bringing them further together. Until she became lost in him, safe to let go and fall into the place he brought them. They might not make sense on paper, but their souls knew each other, somehow understood each other. She arched her back into the pleasure, her toes clenching as she climbed higher and higher, absolutely nothing between them now but this magical, unexplainable connection.

His thrusts grew faster, harder, until they moved together in a perfect rhythm. The musky scent of their sex swept through the air alongside Rhys' woodsy aroma until it all became too much. Too impossible to hold onto. And when he came in a wild rush of deep groans and hard thrusts, he took her over the edge with him.

That's where she stayed, in his arms, in his safety for many, many minutes.

When she finally returned to her body and reopened her eyes, she discovered him staring at her with a sweetness she'd never seen from him before. Nothing was between them anymore. Nothing had ever felt so real before. He saw her, all her faults included, and she saw him. The man behind the mask.

Gaze locked on her, he said roughly, "You said you wanted me."

She nodded slowly, cupping his smooth face. "I did. I do."

He shut his eyes for a moment and breathed in deeply before looking at her again. "There has been no one for a long time. No one I have let in since I lost someone dear to me." Her heart broke, knowing he spoke of his late girlfriend, Katherine, and realizing for the first time that she wasn't the only one with some serious hang-ups. He leaned into her touch and added, "For you, Zoey, there is no pain I wouldn't endure for more time with you."

Every spike in her heart, every lock on it, exploded.

"Rhys," she whispered, beginning to wonder what this meant for them now. "I—"

His kiss promptly cut her off, ending a conversation she knew neither of them was ready for.

CHAPTER 11

The following morning, Rhys was riding a high. The sun was shining brightly outside his office window on Phoenix's main floor. The sky was as clear as the eye could see. Last night had made him...*happy.* A feeling he had not felt in a long time. He hadn't touched a woman on such an intimate level since Katherine, and he'd crossed that line with Zoey last night. It made him remember how good it felt, having a woman at his side. It opened something warm, a closed-off space in his heart. The part of him that had once wanted a wife, a family, and he could see him having those things with Zoey. Going to bed with her every night, waking up next to her in the morning, sharing adventures together. As he continued to stare out the window, he couldn't ignore the truth anymore. He'd crossed the emotional line.

Damn.

"Is this a bad time?"

Rhys blinked and swiveled in his chair away from the window, aware he wasn't alone in his office. Archer stood in the doorway. Rhys waved him in. "Not a bad time at all. What's up?"

Tension creased the corners of Archer's eyes. When he fully entered the office, Rhys understood why. Behind him, Hilary Du Pont, a Phoenix member, made her way through the door. She was the daughter of Gregory Du Pont, the CEO of one of the top tech companies in New York City, and Rhys quickly put two and two together. "Good morning, Hilary."

"Hey," she said in a small voice Rhys had never heard from her before.

Archer gestured to the client chair. After she sat, she bowed her head to her wringing hands. Archer gave Rhys a knowing look and a nod as he took the seat next to her. "Hilary has something she'd like to tell you."

She had yet to look up, so Rhys said as gently as he could, "Hilary, I hope you know you're safe here. Anything you say now will not leave this room."

"I know I'm safe here," she finally said. "It's just really hard for me to say this aloud." She drew in a long, deep breath then looked at Rhys, tears in her eyes. "Jake Grant assaulted me."

Rhys had to control his temper at the brokenness in Hilary's gaze. "When did this happen?"

"Six months ago, at a party," she explained with a shaky voice. "I only had one drink there, but obviously, it was drugged. I woke up in his bed the next day, and he acted like nothing was wrong. I don't remember what happened between us, but I was sore in intimate areas that morning, so something happened."

Sickness roiled through Rhys' gut. He had to keep his feet planted on the ground to ensure he didn't do something stupid and go to Jake's house. The last thing Zoey and Hilary needed were reporters or the police digging into the reason Rhys attacked Jake. "Did you report the incident?" he asked.

A tear slid down her pale cheek. "I told my mother the

morning it happened. She took me to the hospital, but my father talked me out of the rape kit."

Rhys restrained his curses, stretching out his fingers atop his desk not to tighten them into fists. Hilary's shoulders curled, and at that, Rhys rose and moved to the fridge. He offered her a bottle of water. "I'm sorry your father failed you."

Hilary took a quick sip then held the bottle in her lap, her knuckles white. "You know how it is. Your family is probably just the same. A scandal would hurt our name. That's where his thoughts were."

Sadly, Rhys did know how it was. His parents would have buried such a scandal for him too if the situation called for it. A family name meant everything in corporate America, even if that meant hurting a loved one. "So, they told you to be quiet?"

"My father did, yes."

Archer interjected, "But something must have changed. You told Zoey you want to go to the police."

A swift hardness swept over Hilary's face, stealing the weakness from earlier. "Yes, I changed my mind that night Zoey had her first show. The look on her face when she took off her mask. I'm sure no one else realized it, thinking her mask accidentally fell off, but I've seen that look on her face. I see it every time I look in the mirror. And I saw her looking at Jake, and then saw him leave. It wasn't hard to put two and two together." She took another sip of her water. "After I saw that, I hired an investigator to look into it. He showed me Zoey's photograph online and Jake's remarks."

But not Scott's. From the beginning, Rhys had assumed Jake ran this show and Scott got involved in something he should have stopped. He'd seen Scott's guilt when he confronted them. The ghosts following him. Ghosts that Jake did not have. Rhys breathed deeply, controlling what he felt, to keep his head in the right space to help Hilary. He shot Archer a look.

Archer inclined his head, understanding the unsaid statement that Rhys wanted that investigator talked to. Zoey's privacy mattered.

To Hilary, Rhys asked, "Did you know who Jake was behind the mask?"

Hilary nodded. "I did, yes."

"And yet, you've been here at Phoenix with him? Was that not upsetting to you?"

Something haunted crossed her face. "Jake is in my inner circle of friends. I see him every weekend. Avoiding him is impossible. I've just grown to deal with that."

"I'm sorry, Hilary. That must be hard," Rhys said gently.

She lifted a shoulder. "I thought I could handle it, until that night I saw Zoey. After seeing her get justice, I felt shameful that I wasn't strong enough to stand up against him. It made me want to fight back. To prove he had done something terrible to me. That everyone might not know about it, but that I knew, and it didn't break me."

Archer asked, "Is that why you went to see Zoey?"

"Yeah," Hilary replied with a quick nod at him. "I want to tell my story, but I can't do this alone. Who will believe me?"

"I believe you," Rhys said in an instant.

"I do too," Archer agreed.

Hilary's chin quivered. She swallowed deeply before addressing them again, "Thank you. I appreciate that. But I need more than just people believing me. I need another victim. We all know that. I need something more than my word against his."

"You need Zoey's truth," Rhys offered.

Again, Hilary nodded. "Maybe once our stories are out there, more victims will come forward. If there are two of us, there must be more."

Rhys steepled his hands on top of his desk. "I have no doubt there are more victims, but I would ask a favor from you, regarding all this."

She gave him a lopsided grin. "Stay away from Zoey, right?"

Rhys held her gaze, carefully choosing his words. "Whatever you need from me, Hilary, you've got it. Money. Lawyers. Investigators. Contacts. I will help you however I can, but when it comes to Zoey and what she wants out of this, I will protect her at all costs. She's made it clear where she stands on this matter. But if you'd like, Archer can jump on board, and with his resources, he'll help you build a case, as well as possibly find other victims who are more willing to come forward."

Hilary's smile was sweet and soft. "That's more than I can ever ask of you, but if you're offering, I could definitely use the help."

"Then, it's done," Rhys said.

Archer rose, and as Hilary followed, Rhys called, "Does your family know you're planning on coming forward now?"

"No," Hilary said over her shoulder. A powerful hardness in her expression. "I don't particularly care either. I'm done playing by my father's rules."

Rhys inclined his head at her bravery.

However, Archer gave Rhys a look he'd seen before. *We must tread carefully.* The last thing Phoenix needed was Hilary's father finding out about Rhys's and Archer's involvement, which in turn, could expose the club. Rhys never took these risks. But if he could bring hellfire down on Jake, there was no cost he wouldn't pay for what he had done to Zoey. Rhys acknowledged the unsaid between them with a nod. He rose from his desk and leaned against the large double window, staring out again into the sunny day. The sky had been the same on the day Katherine passed away. He remembered that day vividly, the lack of power he felt, and that's what drove him to always be in control now. To help those he could. To bring happiness to those who deserved it. But the one thing he hadn't expected was Zoey and the way she changed him. The way she made him want things he hadn't thought about since Katherine. But the last thing he wanted was for Zoey to lose herself like Katherine did. Zoey didn't want to stay in New York City, the reminder of all she'd been through there, haunting her. How could Rhys ask her to stay for him?

"You deserve her."

Rhys glanced over his shoulder, discovering Archer back in the doorway. His longtime friend had a soft gaze, obviously reading Rhys' thoughts as he added, "Stop punishing yourself for all the things you can't change, Rhys. She's good for you. And you're good for her."

"Let's hope you're right about that," Rhys said.

* * *

Zoey had spent the morning packing up some of her clothes, but by noon, she couldn't stand the familiar lump rising in her throat. She had four clients today, but they were all late-afternoon and evening appointments. Needing to get out, she headed to one of Brooklyn's most beloved cat cafés, The Hungry Kitty. While a part of her was excited to move home to her family in a few weeks, she couldn't stop a question from repeating in her mind: *Why did I meet Rhys now?*

Why couldn't she have met him months ago? Everything felt like it had changed. She didn't feel like the same woman who'd decided to confront Jake and Scott. The woman who wanted to run back to her hometown. She hadn't expected any of this, including how Rhys made her feel. He was a dream come true, a fantasy she didn't know she ever wanted.

And the thought of leaving this new life she'd found made that small lump in her throat a whole lot bigger. Because this wasn't just erotic sex anymore; her heart felt tangled into the mix. Which was precisely why she'd asked Rhys to meet her at the café for a coffee. She could run and hide from her feelings, but she decided to confront them. See if what she felt was real, or if the fantasy of Rhys created feelings that weren't really there.

An older couple strode by, hand in hand, and Zoey smiled at them as her cell phone rang in her purse. One look at the screen had her feeling terrible. Zoey had already missed one call and barely answered two texts. To avoid her mother sending the police over for a wellness check, she picked up. "Hi, Mom."

"She's still alive, thank goodness," her mom joked.

Her mom's voice was sweet and tender and could make Zoey feel better whenever she heard it. "Yup, alive and doing well," she replied, leaning back against the brick wall.

"I hear that. You sound happy. Getting excited to move home?"

"Mm-hmm." Zoey instantly realized her mistake.

Her mom caught on immediately. "That's never a good sound, coming from you. Have you changed your mind?"

Had she? Undecided, Zoey stared out at the cute pug walking its human down the street, across the road, and admitted, "There's just a lot going on right now. I'm excited to move home, but I've also got this life here that's hard to walk away from."

"You can always change your mind about leaving Brooklyn," her mother said gently, the warmth in her voice seeping into the cold spots inside Zoey's chest as she added, "Sometimes you have to test something out to see if it's really what you want. Perhaps this move is happening too fast. You know I selfishly want you home, but we make it work with you out there. Perhaps we can all put more effort into visiting each other, though."

Zoey's throat tightened, confusion making her head hurt. This wasn't the plan. It had never been the plan. Why was she even questioning this? "I miss you, Mom."

"Ah, my darling, we miss you too."

Zoey shut her eyes, guilt nearly drowning her. There were a thousand things she wanted to say to her mother. "Tell me what you've been doing," she asked.

"We've been staying busy, working in the garden. Your father has it in his head that he wants to create a backyard oasis, whatever that means."

Zoey kept her eyes shut and fell into the sweet sound of her mother's voice. The place was safe, where absolutely nothing could touch her.

But then a warm finger stroked her arm. Zoey started and snapped open her eyes, finding Rhys' concerned gaze on her.

"All right?" he mouthed.

Zoey nodded, waiting for her mother to finish her story. "Listen, Mom, I've got to run. I'll call you back when I have a minute. Love you both."

"Sounds good. Love you back, Pumpkin."

The phone line went dead, and Zoey stuck her cell back in her purse. "Sorry about that. I'm okay, just missing my parents, that's all."

"Understandable," he said with a gentle smile. He took a step back then looked up at the sign on the storefront. "So, a cat café, huh?"

She grinned big. "Surprised?"

He sent her a sly smile in return. "Intrigued."

She thought that was a pretty good reaction and whisked the door open. Animals always calmed her, so she figured this was the best place for their first real date. The café was a small rectangular shape with beanbag chairs on the floor and floating tables with wooden benches beneath them. It was her favorite place to visit in Brooklyn.

"Hi, Zoey," Jane said with a wave as she sat behind the counter. "Your usual?"

Zoey turned back to Rhys. "Are you okay with some snacky stuff for lunch? Cheese and meats, that kind of thing, and sweet tea to drink?"

"Sounds great," he said.

Oddly enough, as much as she thought Rhys might look out of place here, he didn't. He really did have the ability of blending in, and yet, he could also stand out like the only man in the room. "Yup, two orders of the usual, please," she called to Jane.

She led him to the far corner, thankful no one else was there today. She sat in the first beanbag chair, and he dropped down into the other. The moment he stretched out his legs, a cat jumped onto his lap.

"Looks like you have a friend," Zoey said.

He smiled down at the orange tabby and petted the cat, who began to purr. "Did you have a lot of pets growing up? Is that where your desire to work in the animal industry comes from?"

"I had as many pets as my parents would allow," she explained with a laugh, reaching out to stroke a passing white cat, who didn't seem interested in Zoey. All the animals at the café were rescues that had been brought in for socialization before finding their forever homes. For as many cats as she could see, there were just as many in hiding spots, too afraid to come out. "I've had a hamster, a couple guinea pigs, and a cat, Oscar, who passed away a few years ago. Did you have any pets?"

Rhys shook his head. "Boarding schools didn't allow pets."

She had assumed he was well educated. "You never went to school here in New York?"

"No," he explained without any emotion in his voice. "That's just the way my family has always done things. For generations."

"I can't imagine not growing up around my family. Did you like boarding school?"

"Loved it," he said with an honest smile. "I'm still in contact with most of the guys I knew from my years there. It's a type of family, I suppose, just different than the one I'm sure you had. But it's never been something I would consider if I had children of my own. I like the idea of having a family life, keeping my children at home with me," his gaze lifted to hers, "and with my wife."

Her heart skipped a little at that. The scariest and most wonderful part was she could imagine a life with Rhys. A happy life. A safe and exciting life. She thwarted any serious talk and shifted the subject. "Can I ask why you got into the whole sex-club thing?" She smiled. "Was it something you aspired to?"

"Funny," he said with a snort, scratching the cat under his chin. "I assume Elise stumbled on the story about my late girlfriend, Katherine."

Zoey cringed. "She did. I'm sorry. I know that's personal, but—"

"It's fair," he interjected. "I knew things about you I shouldn't, because of Archer's vetting." The cat purred louder now as he stroke its back. "Cancer was cruel to Katherine."

"How long did you date her?"

"I met her the second day of college. The cancer came soon after that."

Zoey stroked a long-haired gray-and-white cat that strode by, taking a handful of fur with her. She blew it off her hand. "I'm really sorry, Rhys. I can't even imagine going through that."

He looked at the cat in his lap again, still stroking the

happy feline's back. "It was hard. She hated fate for making her sick. Watching her life end so brutally, with so much anger inside her that she had no control over, taught me no one is getting out of here alive, so you better live your life right." He glanced up at Zoey then held her gaze. "To answer your question, I opened Phoenix because I wanted to be a part of something that gave *more* to people. It also allowed for me to safely indulge in the sensual lifestyle I enjoy, and keep emotionally distant while I grieved. But after a while, something shifted and it became about more than that. Wealth gets you ahead in life, but it doesn't bring you happiness. Sex…" He gave a devilish grin. "Well, I've always lived an erotic lifestyle. Only it used to be in secret with willing participants at private parties. First, in college then out of it." He lifted an easy shoulder, glancing back down at the cat in his lap as he continued stroking him. "Now, I just provide the place and protection for others to indulge too."

She became jealous of that cat purring in his lap. "You know, if you'd have asked me a year ago if that made sense to me, I would have said no. Being so erotic, living that kind of life, was so foreign to me. Now…"

He grinned. "You like it?"

She lifted a shoulder. "It's hard to imagine moving home and never partaking in such things again."

A beat passed. "Who says you have to go anywhere?"

Oh, the loaded question hung in the air, so heavy she could barely breathe. "That was always my plan."

"Plans change," he said with ease, but his eyes told a different story.

She knew she should respond. Have some profound realization, but it never came. The lump in her throat she'd been pushing down rose up again, and her head felt cloudy, making it impossible to think clearly.

Luckily, Jane arrived with lunch, breaking through the

silence. She placed the platter on the small table next to Rhys. "Need anything else, guys?"

Zoey shook her head and gave a smile. "We're good. Thanks, Jane."

Jane smiled in return. "Enjoy."

As she returned to the counter, Rhys blessedly changed the subject, probably for Zoey's benefit. "I thought you might like to know that Archer discovered the woman who came to your shop is a Phoenix member."

"Elise thought that might be the case." Zoey swallowed that lump back down. *Again.* "Is her name really Hilary?"

"It is," Rhys said as the cat purred louder on his lap. "Do you want me to tell you her story?"

Zoey started when a black cat jumped onto the back of the beanbag chair and sat on Zoey's shoulder. She reached up to give the kitty a head scratch. "Is her story similar to mine?"

"Yes, but it's not the part about her assault that I want to tell you."

"Then, what is it?"

"Your bravery was what made her want to come forward."

Zoey quickly looked back at Rhys. His strong gaze held hers. "It wasn't bravery, what I did that night," she countered. "It was the only type of justice I thought I'd ever get. And it was my way out."

"Still brave," he retorted.

She shook her head adamantly as the black cat head-butted her for attention. "No, it's not. It was anger and rage, that's all. Hilary is the one who wants her story out in public. She's the brave one."

Rhys stopped petting the cat and frowned. "Just because you don't want your story told doesn't mean you aren't brave. You confronted the men who assaulted you. Don't undervalue yourself."

She just shrugged as her response. Brave was not hiding anymore. "Is Hilary still going to go to the police?"

Rhys nodded. "That's the plan." At whatever emotion crossed her expression, he quickly added, "But you don't have to worry, she's going to leave you, and your name, out of this. Archer's heading up an investigation now to help her make sure she's got a solid case. If there are more victims, Archer will find them."

"Good," Zoey breathed. "That's good." And yet, she felt like a coward, hiding behind her own fear. But the alternative, going forward, admitting what had happened to her, exposing herself again...

Just as her head began to spin, the black cat swatted Zoey's face before jumping onto her lap. She startled and laughed. "I'm sorry," she said to the cat. "Am I not giving you the attention you deserve?" The cat purred, rubbing his head against Zoey's leg. She hurried to give the animal the scratches he demanded, and he purred even louder.

"If I purr like that, will you stroke me too?"

Zoey shivered at the heat in Rhys' voice. She glanced up into his knowing, devilish smile. It was as if he knew she needed the mood lightened. She didn't know how he did that. Like, he knew exactly how to get her out of her head. Always seemed to say the right thing. To be there for her exactly how she needed him to be there. Be so in tune with her. "Purr, no, but growl? Absolutely."

His eyes flared. "Be careful what you ask for, Zoey."

Like a switch he seemed to control, all the confusion in her mind slowly lifted, his strong stare an anchor where she attached herself. Drawn into him, she leaned forward, bringing her mouth close to his. "Should I be afraid?"

That smile returned, hotter this time. "Depends."

"On?" she breathed.

His gaze greedily scanned over her lips before his smoky

eyes lifted. "If you want me to take you into the bathroom and fuck you."

"You wouldn't do that here." She laughed softly.

He leaned in, heating up the air around her by a few degrees and said, deadly serious, "Try me."

CHAPTER 12

*I*ncredible days had turned into unforgettable weeks. Rhys had spent his days texting Zoey, his evenings getting to know her on dates all over the city, and his nights lost deep inside her, until Rhys' time with Zoey was coming to an end. He'd expected it, but what he didn't expect was how torn he'd become about her leaving. In a couple days, he had to say goodbye to Zoey, and he had no idea how he was going to do that. He hadn't asked if she'd packed. He didn't want to know. Secretly, he kept hoping she'd see the upside to living in New York City, with him. Ever since he'd tossed the idea out to her at the cat café, he'd stayed silent about it, wanting her to make her own choices, but staying quiet was slowly killing him.

When he stepped out of the shower, ready to start his day, he was certain nothing could make matters worse for him and Zoey, but he was wrong. "Turn on the news," Archer said by way of greeting after Rhys answered his cell phone.

"What's going on?" he asked, wrapping a towel around his waist and heading back into his bedroom.

"Just turn on the news, Rhys," Archer said, solemnly.

Rhys grabbed the remote off his nightstand and turned the television on. In an instant, he completely understood the heaviness in Archer's voice. Splashed across the screen: *Wall Street broker Scott Ross has died by suicide.* "When did this happen?" Rhys demanded.

"Details are scarce at the moment, but looks like some-time last night," Archer reported.

Rhys read the headline, trying to weed through all his thoughts. "How sure are they that this is a suicide?" Scott had felt remorse. Jake hadn't. Rhys knew when pressed into a tight corner, people did terrible things.

"My thoughts went there, too, but Hunt is working the case. He told me this morning that it's an open-and-shut case. Scott left a suicide note, cleaned up all his finances for his family; he was very methodical about it all."

Only one thing mattered to Rhys. "Did he name Zoey in his note?"

"Not that I'm aware of. He only stated that some wrongs could never be forgiven and he was tired of living a lie."

Rhys snorted. "Well, he wasn't wrong."

"Agreed," Archer said. "I'll reach out if anything further develops."

"Appreciate it." Rhys ended the call and headed straight for his closet. Only one person was on his mind now. How would Zoey react to this news? Just the thought had him quickly throwing on jeans and a t-shirt and making his way to his front door, grabbing his keys and wallet off the small table.

In quick time, he reached the parking garage and sped out in his sports car. Zoey's place was far, and with traffic, it took him longer than he would have liked to arrive at the loft on the shipyard. Every minute, every second, feeling like a life-time. A phone call to Zoey was faster but would be impersonal, and certainly not how Rhys wanted to break the news. He needed Zoey in his arms. After he found a parking spot, he sprinted through the building and knocked on her door, only belatedly realizing how early it was. A quick look at his watch revealed it was seven thirty. But when the door whisked open and he caught sight of Hazel's sad eyes, he knew he hadn't gotten here fast enough.

"Zoey?" he asked.

"She's in here." Hazel opened the door wider.

Rhys found Zoey sitting on the couch, her legs pulled up tight to her chest, her red-rimmed eyes locked on the news. He made it inside in three large strides, and the moment he got close, Zoey's eyes landed on him. Something in his chest broke, yanking him forward until he dropped to his knees in front of her. "Don't look at me that way. Do you hear me, Zoey?"

Her chin quivered. Tears welled in her sweet eyes. "I did this to him."

"No," he said firmly, taking her shaky hands in his. "This is not on you. Scott did this to himself."

"If you need us, we'll just be in my room."

Rhys recognized Elise's voice from behind him, but he never looked back. He couldn't look away from the dark despair on Zoey's face, the blame heavy in her features. A feeling he understood intimately, one he'd felt for a long time after Katherine died when he could do nothing to save her. But Zoey wasn't Katherine, and Rhys was ready to battle this storm. "Talk to me," he said, cupping her face.

She leaned into his hold, her eyes fluttering shut. "I just can't stop thinking about that night you confronted him. He looked so remorseful." Her sad eyes met his again and held. "When he apologized, it was clear he was haunted by what he'd done."

"He should have been haunted," Rhys reminded her

gently, holding her face tightly, keeping her attention wholly on him. "That guilt was his to bear. And only his."

"Maybe." Her chin quivered. "Maybe not. I wanted justice, but I never wanted to destroy him."

He wanted to remind her that Scott had destroyed her for a long time without any care, but that wouldn't help. To be so cold wasn't in her heart. And he cherished that about her. He joined her on the couch, gathering her in his arms, close to him. When he rested his chin on the top of her head, he said, "Feel what you feel right now, but tomorrow let that go. This isn't on you, Zoey."

"Then, why does it feel like it is," she cried.

He locked his arms around her, wishing he could bear this for her. Hell, he wished he could take all of this away. Furthermore, he wished he could take away anything in the future that would hurt her. He dropped his lips to her head, and the sweet vanilla of her shampoo infused the air. Speaking from personal experience, he offered, "Life has many, many dark moments, and you can't run from those, but you don't need to face this alone. What do you need from me?"

"Just this," she said, her voice small.

He tightened his arms further, hoping, praying, this would somehow ease her suffering. With the warmth of her body against him, washed with vulnerability and sadness, he had to shut his eyes against the familiarity. Against the moment when he was powerless to help someone in pain. He thought he could avoid this feeling forever. Would run if he ever felt it again.

He didn't run.

He stayed.

"Tell me what you're thinking," he eventually said, breaking the long silence.

She paused, a heavy pause. When she spoke again, he

couldn't hear tears in her voice. "I'm thinking that this was not the outcome I wanted. I just wanted to feel better, you know? I didn't want my actions to end in someone's death."

His stomach turned, and he locked his arms around her. "Your actions didn't result in someone's death. Scott's actions did." He leaned away to tip her chin up to him, meeting her despondent stare. "People make their choices. You made yours. Good things will come from that. Scott made his. His weren't good choices; nothing good can come from that."

Her eyes searched his. "You think Scott deserved this fate?"

"Yes."

She held his stare for a beat. "No one deserves death."

"But death happens regardless," he countered. "It's coming for all of us." Rhys knew that lesson. He'd seen death rip apart Katherine until all the good in her was gone, replaced by anger that her life was cut short. So many dreams unmet. So many needs and wants unfulfilled. He brushed Zoey's hair away from her face, tucking it behind her ear. "You can let this consume you, or you can realize that none of this is in your control. Not what Scott and Jake did to you. Not their responses to it." He had never crossed the line he was about to cross, but he crossed it easily now. "I'd like to show you something. Will you come somewhere with me?"

Her eyes searched his. He swore she nearly said, *I'll go anywhere with you.* Instead, she said, "Okay, yeah."

They wasted no time getting in his car, and they stayed silent on the long drive back into Manhattan, through morning traffic. When he pulled into the cemetery, he caught the moment when Zoey went statue-still. He drove up the hill and around the slight corner before he pulled over beside Katherine's grave then got out. Zoey followed him, stopping next to him, as he stared down at her gravestone.

He hoped what he said next would have an impact.

Helped even a little. "I loved Katherine. Loved her more than I thought I could love anyone. She was everything I wanted in a woman. She was caring, fun, and had such a zest for life." His throat tightened, but he breathed deeply again, pushing back the emotion to get through this. "Until her cancer diagnosis." Zoey's warm fingers tangled with his, her other hand wrapping around his forearm, as he continued, "I never would have believed what happened after that. The way Katherine changed."

"Changed, how?" Zoey asked gently.

Rhys kept his focus on the tombstone. It had a slight purple tone, Katherine's favorite color. "You always see inspirational stories about cancer. The way a person fights so bravely for their life. Katherine tried to fight for a while, but the cancer was aggressive. Chemo couldn't even touch it. She got so sick."

"I'm so sorry, Rhys," Zoey said, tears in her voice.

He couldn't look her way, couldn't get through this if he did. "The plan had been to do surgery once the tumors shrunk, but the chemo wasn't shrinking the tumors. They were getting bigger." His throat tightened. His breathing became hard. He shut his eyes, relieving the look of rage that had crossed Katherine's face. "The day the doctor told Katherine there was nothing they could do for her, she changed. The light in her went out."

"She gave up?"

Rhys gave Zoey a quick look, finding warm compassion staring back at him. "Not only gave up, but anger stole the Katherine I knew and loved. She couldn't see the good in anything. She lived for another two months, and she became a shell of the woman she was. She wouldn't come outside. She wouldn't talk to any of her friends. She sat in a dark room and stayed there."

Zoey squeezed his fingers. "That must have been hard to watch."

Rhys nodded, exhaled deeply, and looked at the tombstone. "I couldn't reach her. I couldn't help her. I could do nothing to save her. But worst of all, I couldn't find my way back to her. When she died, she screamed in a way that will forever haunt me. There was no peace, no love, only rage." He glanced sideways at Zoey. "I know what you've gone through is horrible. Inconceivable. But don't do what Katherine did. Don't let something consume you until all that you are, all that makes you, *you*, is gone. Promise me that."

He wasn't sure what showed on his face, but she quickly threw her arms around him, holding him tight. "I promise, Rhys," she whispered. "I promise."

* * *

"You'll call me if you need me?" Rhys asked, standing at Zoey's front door after they returned from the cemetery.

She was still processing everything he had told her. But the one thing that stayed with her was that Rhys made a whole lot of sense to her now. He'd seen someone die before their death. That had to change a person on every level. More importantly, Rhys was no longer a fantasy. Not anymore. The only thing she saw, even now, staring into the strength of his eyes, was a man to adore. A man she didn't want to walk away from. "I'll call, I promise," she said.

She expected him to kiss her. He surprised her by gathering her in his arms, holding her tight, and dropping a firm kiss onto her forehead, the most tender thing he'd done yet. She knew by the locking of his arms that he didn't want to let go. Part of her didn't want him to either.

When he finally leaned away, a pillar of strength, as always, he said, "No matter the time, I'm here for you. All right?"

She gave a small smile, hoping he saw the honest gratitude at his sharing his story with her, something obviously incredibly painful. "Thank you. I appreciate that."

He simply nodded and released her, although she could see it pained him to do so. As he headed back to his car, she watched him. Fate was a funny thing. Without Katherine's death, Phoenix never would have happened. Without the assault, she wouldn't have met Rhys. Without a doubt, both of their trauma and pain shaped them. She couldn't help but wonder if all this was meant to be, and that made her head hurt more.

"He went home?"

Zoey glanced over her shoulder to find Hazel and Elise standing in the doorway, doing a not-so-great job at hiding. "Yeah," Zoey said, turning around to face them. "I thought it was a good idea to have some time alone to process all that's happened."

"You want to be alone?" Hazel said, solemnly.

"Not alone, *alone*." They moved out of the way, and Zoey stepped inside, sliding her arm through Hazel's. "But more like, alone with you, the two greatest friends a girl could ask for."

"Okay, phew." Hazel smiled a little, giving Zoey's arm a tug and leading her down the hallway. Once inside her bedroom, Zoey climbed in the middle of her queen-size platform bed while Hazel and Elise sank in on either side, the mattress bouncing beneath them. Boxes filled the room, no evidence that Zoey loved her life with Elise and Hazel. The flower-patterned duvet was crumpled from the night before, a reminder of the hurry in which Zoey had gotten out of bed after Elise told her what happened to Scott.

Silence settled in, a comfortable one. She could feel their curious stares on her and figured she'd answer the unsaid questions. "You're wondering what I'm thinking, right?"

Hazel's soft voice drifted over to her as she patted Zoey's arm. "We don't want to push you. Share if you want to, but we can also just cuddle. You know how I love to cuddle."

"I do know that," Zoey said, smiling over at Hazel. She gave the best hugs. "Honestly, I don't even know where my head is at right now, other than I'm feeling sad. Sad any of this has happened. It's weird, you know?" She turned her head toward Elise. "I've thought about Scott every day for the past year. His existence was there in my head all the time, and now he's just...*gone.* I think I'm having trouble reconciling that."

Elise gave a soft nod in understanding. "You've got a lot to process, but if you ask me, that guy got what was coming to him."

"He sure as hell did," Hazel agreed. When Zoey looked at her in surprise, Hazel shrugged. "I know I'm not usually one to wish harm on anyone, but we all answer to someone. Scott's choices could only lead him down one path."

Zoey leaned her head back against her pillow and closed her eyes, letting the quiet darkness fall over her. "Rhys said that same thing, and I know you're all right, but when Rhys confronted them, Scott apologized to me. It felt sincere."

"Yeah, but the thing is," Elise countered. "That was an apology for you, not for him. Maybe he was trying to right a wrong to make you feel better. I imagine he lost all the good parts of his soul when he stood by and let what happened to you happen, and that's what drove him to do what he did."

The thought of anyone being in that much pain had Zoey fighting back tears, her throat squeezing up tight. "But isn't that sad? How long does someone have to pay for something they've done wrong?"

Elise's voice turned harsh. "Forever, Zoey, because that's how long you have to deal with it too."

With that statement, Elise had made things very clear. Zoey opened her eyes and glanced between her friends. "Yeah, but I don't want to deal with this forever," she acknowledged.

Hazel and Elise exchanged a worried look before Elise said firmly, "You're not thinking of hurting yourself."

"Of course not," said Zoey, taking her friends' hands and squeezing tightly. "I've always known I had to keep going, no matter what. But, I guess, after that picture came out, I was on autopilot, just trying to survive what had happened. I kind of just took one step in front of the other to keep moving forward, but then I met you two, and everything changed."

"Because we love you," Hazel said.

Elise smiled. "We do, so much."

"And I love you both too." Zoey smiled as well, the same lump rising in her throat again. "At the same time, I think that's what is so confusing. You see, we had a plan. Get my type of justice against Jake and Scott at Phoenix. That's what drove us for a while."

Elise caught on. "But then things changed?"

"Everything changed," Zoey agreed with a nod. "After my night at Phoenix, I thought I'd walk away and move home with the money I needed to get my life back on track. But ever since that night, every time I think about leaving, I get this lump in my throat. I know that's because I don't want to move away. I don't want to leave either of you."

"Then, don't go," Hazel implored.

Elise squeezed Zoey's hand tightly. "If we've given you the impression that we want you to go, I'm sorry. We really want you to stay, but we thought you needed our support. That's all."

Zoey's voice quivered. "I did need your support, but I don't think it's as simple as wanting to stay or leave. I'm not sure I have a choice in the matter."

Elise pushed up, giving a fierce stare. "You have a choice in everything, Zoey."

If only it were that easy. "To a point, I agree with you. I had the choice to walk through Phoenix's doors. I had the choice to take Rhys up on his offer to spend more time with him. I even had the choice to cross over that line and let my heart get tangled up in this wild fantasy I've been living."

Hazel's brows drew together. "I'm waiting for the bad in all this. Rhys is a total catch."

"Which is exactly the problem," Zoey said. "He *is* a catch. I wasn't supposed to feel like this. Because no matter how good things are right now, the truth remains, what happened with Jake and Scott is never going away. No matter what I do. No matter that there is so much good in my life at the moment." She smiled between them. "I've got these two best friends who mean the world to me. I've got this amazing guy showing me this incredible life I never would have believed existed. I'm actually trusting people again. I'm feeling things I refused to let myself feel before. And yet, hanging over all that, is the constant reminder that, in a split second, everything can go wrong. Here, in New York City, I cannot escape what happened. I fear taking the subway. I'm terrified to accept a drink I don't see poured in front of me. It feels like there is no escape."

Elise's expression said: *Don't escape. Fight against it.* Of course, she never spoke those words aloud. Elise wouldn't. That wasn't her style. Instead, her friend gave her a knowing look. "Just trust in yourself and your judgment. You've got this. And no matter what happens, if you decide to stay or leave, we'll be here for you."

Zoey did the last thing she thought she'd do today. She

smiled. And then fell into the warm embrace of the two friends who'd brought her back from the darkest time in her life.

$\mathcal{R}$hys woke up irritated, and the mood stayed with him for the remainder of his day, including through his dinner business meeting. Ever since Katherine, Rhys had stuck to the rules, lived by a moral code, and never broke away from that. He knew the risks with Zoey when he began breaking rules for her, but he hadn't anticipated where his heart would be at the end of their time together. But now he knew. He didn't want her to leave. He wanted to keep exploring this amazing thing they had going on. He knew there was something special about her the night he met her, and he'd been fooling himself into believing he controlled any of this. It didn't matter if a day had passed, or a month, or a year, he wanted *her*.

Needing to get his head on straight, he called the guys over. The men currently sitting around him on his patio next to the pool had been there when Katherine died. They'd all seen him break down and cry. For the last hour, he admitted everything. Including that, while throwing out his rule book for Zoey, he'd also throw her his heart.

"Fight for her," Archer said, sitting across from Rhys.

The sparkling lights of New York City glistened across the dark sky behind him, but any light in Rhys felt diminished. "It's not that easy."

"Why?" Kieran asked, a glass of whiskey resting on his thigh. "It is that simple, isn't it? Ask her to stay. Ask her to move in. Make it a big deal for her, she'll like that."

"And then what happens after I do that?" Rhys countered. "I tell her to stay in the one place where she is reminded constantly of what happened to her? She doesn't trust New York City. Her fear lives here."

Hunt, who'd been relatively quiet so far, said, "Then, make it safe for her. Do whatever you have to do. Tell her that nothing will touch her in this city. Not when she's with you, and while you're at it, you get that fucker, Jake, put behind bars."

Rhys wanted to do all that and so much more. "I can't make that choice for her, and you all fucking know it." He grabbed the whiskey glass and polished off his drink, embracing the burn in his throat. "If I did, I could expect one outcome. That she'd lose herself like Katherine did. That she'd change and morph into a person who could survive being here. She'd push all that trauma down for me. I can't do that to her. I won't. She has to decide this for herself."

A telling silence descended onto the patio. One filled with a hard truth—Rhys had no control here. He rubbed his face, easing the twitchiness of his extremities. Then he focused on Archer, hoping he could look at this through a different angle. "Has anything further come from helping Hilary?"

Archer shook his head, reaching for his glass of scotch on the coffee table. Before he took a sip, he answered, "Not yet. It won't be a quick process. Hilary found Zoey by chance. Finding other victims won't be so easy. There's no obvious trail on the web, like there was with Zoey. It's a tiresome process, and an invasion of privacy since Hilary will have to make contact the same way she did with Zoey."

"Stay with it," Rhys countered. "If there is a way for me to get this handled without directly involving Zoey, then that's the path to take. The only plan forward is getting Jake out of the picture so New York City feels safe to her again." To Hunt, he added, "Any word on Scott's suicide?"

"Nothing much there, except that it's officially been ruled a suicide," Hunt replied.

Kieran's head whipped around to Rhys. "You suspected foul play?"

Rhys shrugged. "I would not have put it past Jake if he thought Scott would oust him."

"He's dirty enough to do it," Archer agreed, swirling the ice in his drink.

"Possibly," Hunt said after a moment of consideration. "But there was no evidence in Scott's apartment of foul play and tons of evidence pointing to suicide. Coroner has ruled it a suicide, and the case is closed."

On one hand, that was good news. If Scott's life was investigated, no doubt Zoey's story would come out. On the other hand, Jake still roamed free in New York City. Rhys blew out a frustrated breath and reached for the whiskey bottle, pouring himself another shot as his cell phone rang. After he answered, his condo's security said, "There is a Ms. Parker to see you."

"Send her up," Rhys said, ending the call and sliding his cell back onto the glass coffee table. "Zoey's on her way up."

Archer rose. "And that's our cue to leave."

Rhys threw back the shot, appreciating the warmth in his veins, the lessening of the tension in his chest. "Thanks for dropping by and being a sounding board."

Hunt slapped Rhys on the back. "We've got you, buddy. You know that."

Yeah, Rhys did.

They said their goodbyes after that, and Rhys stayed on the patio furniture and watched them leave through the tall windows of his condo. Before Archer headed out the front door, he opened it a little wider, and Zoey entered. She wore jeans and a dark-green blouse, the same color as the lingerie she'd worn the first night he met her. She exchanged words with Archer and a short laugh, then her gaze flicked to the windows. She nodded at Archer before she headed toward the patio doors.

The second she stepped outside, Rhys knew he was going to hate what came out of her mouth.

"Hey."

The single word had never sounded so sad.

He remained rooted to the couch as she slowly walked toward him, her hair fluttering in the warm breeze. Christ, she was the most beautiful woman he'd ever seen.

She stopped in front of him, regret in her gaze. "I—"

"Need to move home," he finished for her, his voice barely controlled. He wanted to beg her to stay. To not leave him. But New York City was toxic to her, and he couldn't be a part of the problem. He'd seen Katherine fade away into nothing. This environment, maybe seeing Jake at functions she'd come to with Rhys, would do just that to her. He couldn't watch her fade away. Zoey needed to flourish.

Something he could see written all over her face when she said in a small voice, "This is a really confusing thing because I don't really want to leave. There's Hazel and Elise, and...*you.*"

He rose, moving close, drawn to her. All along, the plan had been for her to go, but now, the plan was blown to shit. Because he knew one thing for certain: her heart was meant for him. "You deserve to go home and start over, Zoey."

She took a step forward, bringing herself even closer. "I didn't expect to feel like this."

The warm breeze fluttered around them as he cupped her face. "Feel like what?"

"I don't want to leave you," she said so easily.

That's what caught him up too. Things between them were too easy. Too real. Too right. "I never expected this either. Never expected I would want you to stay."

She gave a lopsided smile. "And yet here we are."

He smiled gently, not wanting to put his own wants on her. "But this also isn't goodbye either, just like I'm sure it's not goodbye with Hazel and Elise. You can visit, can you not?"

"Yes, I can visit."

But it won't be enough echoed in the space between them.

She added, "And you can come see me, too."

"Easily done," he agreed. *But I'll never want to leave.*

Every word he spoke felt odd coming from his mouth. He wanted her here. With him. To see every day. To kiss. To make love to. To laugh with. To explore. To enjoy. Anything else felt...*wrong.*

She tipped her head back, hitting him with those warm, affectionate eyes. Their gazes held for a beat. "I won't ever forget what you did for me, Rhys."

He gathered her in his arms and pressed a kiss to the top of her head, feeling like the moment she left him tonight, she'd take his heart with her. And with that realization, Rhys knew Archer was right. No matter what, Rhys had to fight for her. "I will never forget you either, Zoey."

Desperate to hold onto her for as long as he could, he dropped his mouth to hers. Her lips molded to his in a gentle kiss, but when he angled her head and deepened his embrace, he knew everything had changed. That he had changed, and she was the reason for it.

Needing to get closer to her, he gathered her in his arms and brought her inside, into his bedroom, laying her out on his king-size bed. He knew they weren't done. Not even close. He knew that, even if she walked away, he'd chase her. And with a slight amusement, he understood what he should have known all along: he still wasn't done breaking rules for Zoey.

He hovered over her, the lights from the skyscrapers outside his window casting a warm glow across her face. She leaned her head up, offering herself and fisting her hands on his shirt. "Don't wait."

The same urgency rushed through him as he hurried to get her naked. Between the hot kisses, he removed his shirt and she had his pants down and was yanking him forward with her hands caressing his ass. He went willingly, lifting her legs up underneath his arms as he slid deep inside her. He groaned, resting his forehead against hers. She was tight, wet, and he wanted to stay there forever. "How are you so fucking perfect, Zoey?"

"Rhys," she said, her voice nearly begging.

He lifted his head, met the desire burning in her eyes, and began moving slowly, letting her feel every single inch of him. There was no show tonight. No star. No one else watching. Only her and him, and yet this was the most intimate, addictive sex he'd ever had.

Every brush of her lips against his, the way she hugged him, he couldn't possibly get enough. Her breasts were soft beneath his chest, her moans the only sound registering. She smelled like vanilla and ripe woman, and he was certain the scent was handmade for him. He leaned against her legs, lifting her bottom higher, and thrust his hips, burying himself deep without any barrier between them. Her soul shone through her eyes, and his reached out, encasing her entirely, and he knew he had one final rule to break. He wanted breakfast in the mornings. He wanted her soft curves next to him when he went to sleep. He wanted *this.* Always. Just them. He wanted to hear her laugh. He needed her arms around him on tough days. He wanted to hear more of her stories and understand the way her heart worked.

Passion drove him to thrust harder, faster, until she moved with him and they set a rhythm that blended their moans. Skin slapped against skin as he filled her, took all of what she offered him, and he still wanted more. Her nails dug into his back as her feet locked on his thighs, her drenched sex constructing with every thrust.

Tighter...tighter...wetter... And when her screams of ecstasy washed over him, he went nearly cross-eyed at the pleasure her body gave him. He thrust forward, coming with a roar and emptying himself inside her. He knew nothing from this night on would ever be the same again.

And that's exactly how he wanted it.

CHAPTER 14

*N*ine days had passed since Zoey moved back to Sacramento. Each day felt longer than the last. She had turned on autopilot the moment she got on the plane to come home. She'd only brought a few suitcases and still hadn't arranged for a moving company to bring her boxes home. *Slow.* That's how she'd been taking all this. One step then another until her head wasn't so cloudy and making decisions was easier. Knowing it wasn't going to happen tonight, she grabbed the bowl of popcorn off her parents' kitchen counter and headed for the living room.

Her childhood house was a gorgeous two-story Victorian on the corner of Meadow Lane. Her parents had bought the property when Zoey was only two years old, and they'd spent Zoey's entire life renovating it from top to bottom. Zoey's favorite part of the house was the living room with the old stone fireplace and big bay window, where her mother always put up the Christmas tree. Only this time, as she entered the living room and found her dad sitting in his usual recliner, something felt off. Wrong. She kept thinking that, after she moved home, she'd feel more settled. But that lump in her throat was baseball-size now, and she could no longer swallow it away. She felt tired and edgy, not sleeping much, missing Hazel and Elise…missing Rhys and the new life she'd discovered with him.

Trying not to drown in her confusion, she tossed a piece of popcorn into her mouth. "Whatcha watching tonight?"

"Unsolved Mysteries," her dad said, flashing her a smile. Though, at the moment, a news story was on.

He'd always been a handsome man. Fit and healthy, her father looked closer to forty than his actual age of fifty. He had blond hair that barely showed his grays, and light-blue eyes that always lit up when her mother came around.

And they presently glistened as her mom entered the room, carrying a big bag of salt and vinegar chips; her dad's favorite. "Don't eat the whole bag," she mused.

Her dad just smiled. "Thank you, honey." He promptly dove into his chips, his attention turned back to the television.

Her mom shook her head at him and sent Zoey a soft, sweet smile as she sat on the couch. She had a short bob, the same strawberry-blond color as Zoey's. But her mother's eyes were brown. Zoey got the hazel from her grandmother. "Find yourself a guy who is this easy to make happy." Whatever crossed Zoey's face, warmed her mother's smile. "Was Rhys like that?"

Zoey had told her parents all about Rhys. Well, minus the part where he owned a sex club. She kept enough secrets from her parents, and Rhys was too incredible to be a secret. "He never really asked for anything." *But he gave so much back.* Zoey's heart swelled, feeling fuzzy in all the right places. Rhys hadn't really asked for anything at all. He'd simply been there for her. She understood why now, of course. He couldn't bear to watch anyone lose themselves like Katherine had lost herself. And yet…*and yet*…over the last days she'd been without him, she felt lost. "That's what's really so great about him," Zoey added, diving her hand back into the bowl of popcorn. "He's a very selfless guy."

Her mom smiled. "He's a good one, then. Is he planning to come out and visit?"

They had talked every day since she moved. They texted often. "I don't really know. We haven't discussed it much." Rhys, while affectionate and warm, hadn't spoken about what came next for them.

"Bet he's got a plan," her dad said.

Zoey lifted her brows at her father. "What makes you say that?"

He glanced over with his clever smile. "If he hasn't talked to you about what's happening next, he's figuring it out and forming a plan. That's how men work."

"What plan could he possibly be forming?" Zoey countered. "I left him in New York City."

Her dad stuffed his hand in the bag of potato chips and focused back on the television. "I'm no psychic, Zoey. I'm just telling you how men work. They don't discuss things. They make a plan and execute it."

"Well, I don't know about that," her mom said to him. To Zoey, she added, "If it's meant to be, honey, then it will be. No sense fretting about it."

Zoey agreed with a nod, falling right back into autopilot. "I do know that Elise and Hazel are planning to come visit soon. You'll finally get to meet them."

Her mom's eyes lit up. "Oh, that's wonderful." She reached for the yarn and her crochet hook in the basket next to her. She made blankets for all the new babies who came to her practice. Zoey had once imagined doing that for the sick animals when she became a vet. The lump in her throat felt impossible to swallow once more, and she took a long sip of her sweet tea, as her mom said, "You've had all these people in your life, and it's been so strange not to know any of them."

Truth was, Zoey had meant it that way. She'd kept everyone at a safe, comfortable distance. Her home life and her life in New York City had been a world apart, and that's how she liked it. Blending the two felt dangerous.

"Any luck on the house hunt today?" her dad asked.

Zoey shook her head, nibbling on a popcorn kernel. "Nothing feels quite right."

"Ah, you'll find something soon," he said. "Just needs to be the right house."

He turned back to the television, and the sound of crunching potato chips had Zoey smiling. He was totally going to eat that whole bag. The only plan she had made was to get into Phoenix, get the money, and come home. But being home wasn't working. It felt good to stay with her parents; everything was so familiar and warm. But at home, her friends weren't there. Rhys wasn't there. Her life wasn't here. And no matter how many houses she and her mother looked at, none of them were a good fit. Everything felt wrong, and that made no sense.

With a sigh, she shoved a handful of popcorn into her mouth, tasting too much salt, and watched the news, grateful for something to distract her thoughts. A breaking-news report caught Zoey's attention. The female reporter said, "The I80 rapist has been arrested earlier tonight, our sources tell us."

"Oh, thank goodness they found him." Her mom turned to Zoey and explained, "You probably didn't hear about this in New York City, but for the last couple weeks, this evil person has been terrorizing women along the I80. He set up a trap at truck stops and kidnapped them."

"Those poor women," Zoey said, a slow coldness beginning to creep into her veins.

"Good police work," her dad commented. He clicked off the news report and turned on Unsolved Mysteries.

The person being interviewed on the show said, "There were so many warnings. So many signs, so many incidents. Had we been paying attention earlier, it would have been obvious Carl was dangerous, but no one spoke up."

Zoey felt the walls begin to creep in on her. The two stories were completely unrelated to each other, but they felt intimately connected to her. Like the world was trying to tell her something.

This time, she listened.

Scott was gone, but Jake wasn't. He still lived in Manhattan, still hadn't changed if he assaulted Hilary and showed absolutely no remorse. What if Jake escalated and turned into a rapist that kidnapped women? What if he'd already done that? He'd been so cold when he knew she was watching. The arrogance and hatred had been blinding. With a cold shiver, her heart asked: *What if your silence hurt another woman? What if he becomes more violent and kills someone? What if you could stop it?*

"Honey, are you okay?"

Zoey blinked, only then aware of the moisture on her cheeks. Her breath caught, air impossible to breathe in. She'd been so afraid of the truth she had buried deep inside her, ashamed of what happened. That, somehow, it had been her fault, and that the shame would destroy her. But it occurred to her now, sitting in the warm comfort of her childhood home, alongside her parents, that Rhys was right. She couldn't let what Scott and Jake did change her. She couldn't let them dim her light or her truth. She couldn't lose herself like Katherine had lost herself. But she had done just that; she'd let them win. *Again.* She left a life she loved, a man who was opening her heart in ways she only dreamed of, all because fear ate at her like a disease.

With shaky hands, she reached for her purse sitting on the floor next to her and took out Hilary's card that she hadn't been able to throw away.

"Zoey," her dad said, firmer now, sliding closer to her on the couch. "What's wrong?"

"Mom," Zoey managed, glancing between them. "Dad." A sob broke free. "I need to tell you something."

* * *

"WILLIAM," Rhys said to his cousin, frustration coursing through him. "I don't want to hear how this is a terrible idea. I need you to tell me the steps I have to take to make sure I'm good to leave for Sacramento." They sat across from each other in the cigar lounge, on the brown leather couches, with a glass coffee table between them. Even if they were related, William looked nothing like Rhys. He was tall and lanky, with light features, and five years younger. The bar wouldn't open until later this afternoon, but Rhys had business he needed to take care of. The bartenders were already there, restocking the bars and handling the day-to-day chores.

Next to the pile of paperwork was the plane ticket that would take him to Sacramento tonight at eight o'clock. He'd done the right thing, letting Zoey leave, to choose her own path. But it made him miserable. Rhys didn't have a plan, not fully, but he knew he couldn't take the distance between them. He could not ask her to stay, and he knew she'd never ask him to go, but fuck, he needed to see her again. This life without her was not one he could survive.

"I realize you want me to rush this," William shot back. "But this isn't something I can do so quickly. You oversee a lot of your family's investments. And let's not even talk about your own finances." The color drained out of his face. "I

149

don't even know where to begin on this. You are the face of the Harrington fortune here in New York City."

Rhys knew if he left New York City, he'd shake things up. He needed to have this all squared away. Because he knew once he got to Sacramento, there was no chance in hell he'd leave again. "I know I'm dropping all this into your lap, but I've got total trust that you can handle things here in New York until we figure out how to make all this work."

William shot a look of disbelief. "Fuck, Rhys, I am not you. You've got meetings scheduled for the next month. You honestly want to bail on those?" He blinked twice. "Okay, what the hell is going on? Are you having a mental breakdown? Do you need help? I can get that for you."

Rhys had never been so certain about anything before. And yet, he understood William's concern. Rhys never acted impulsively. But time and time again, Zoey made him break his own rules. He leaned his elbows on his bent knees. He couldn't tell his cousin the reason he was leaving was for Zoey. That news would get to his father. And the last thing he wanted was for Zoey to be the target of his father's wrath for being the reason he left his responsibilities behind. Rhys knew how to thwart his father. Zoey did not. "My sanity is fine. Reschedule important meetings over Zoom. Go to dinner meetings on my behalf." Because that's how finance worked. Schmooze the right people. Keep contacts and close relationships tight. Let them know how sweet it was to be in the Harrington circle.

William blinked. "Have you talked to your father about this?"

"I don't need to discuss my plans with anyone," Rhys countered.

William paled a little, shuffling through the papers. "All right, all right. Shit, all right." A bead of sweat slid down the side of William's cheek. He gave Rhys a look of disbelief.

"You're planning on running your life in New York from Sacramento? This is insane."

"What's insane?"

Rhys glanced sideways, realizing that Archer, Hunt, and Kieran had arrived. Rhys had hoped to have his conversation with William wrapped up before then. "Give us a minute," he told William, who looked slightly wobbly as he rose.

"I'll go have a drink at the bar," his cousin said. He nodded a greeting to Rhys' friends before leaving the sitting area.

Kieran chuckled at the retreating William. "What did you do to him? He looks ready to puke."

Rhys exhaled deeply as they all took seats around him. This was the hardest part. "I wanted to wait to tell you all this until I had everything lined up, but I'm moving to Sacramento."

The silence was deafening.

Rhys chuckled. "I don't think I've ever rendered you all speechless before."

Archer countered, "I don't think you've ever hit us with such a bombshell before. When did you decide this?"

"It's been in the works since the night Zoey told me she was leaving," he explained, hating the sadness he noted in his friends' eyes. "It's not an easy decision for me. I didn't come to it lightly, but you're right, I need to fight."

"For her?" Hunt offered.

Rhys nodded. "She can't do New York City, and understandably so, but I can do Sacramento. It's just going to take some planning."

Archer cocked his head. "She's the one, then?"

"I think we all knew that from day one." Rhys smiled. "Listen, I've got a big ask, but I'll be renting my condo, and I'll need to hire a manager to oversee the cigar club. Archer, you can handle Phoenix until we get someone to step in my place. We'll have to look at this from all angles, but—"

"Let me stop you there," Hunt said, offering his typical sly smile. "You know we've got your back and would help you figure all this out, but I really hate to break it to you, buddy; you're not going anywhere."

Rhys tipped his head back and let out a frustrated breath. "Please do not give me a hard time about this. It's not easy to leave any of you." He dropped his chin and glanced between his friends. "But this is happening. I'm leaving tonight."

Hunt's smile widened. "While I've totally got the warm fuzzies over the love fest you're showing us, what I mean is, you're not going anywhere, because an arrest warrant was just filed for Jake. Zoey flew back to New York City with her parents to speak out against him this morning. Between Hilary's statement and Zoey's, it was enough to press charges."

Rhys rose, thrusting his hands in his hair. He moved to the window and cracked it open to get some fresh air, hardly able to believe what he'd heard. Delight filled him that she was facing her fears head-on and testifying against Jake. He'd been so worried she lost herself like Katherine did, but he'd never been happier to be wrong. He shut his eyes and breathed deeply, gathering his thoughts, then he glanced back over his shoulder. "She came forward?"

Hunt nodded with a warm smile. "She came forward."

Ten minutes ago, he was ready to walk away from New York City and go to Zoey. The plane ticket was bought. His plan set. Of course she'd completely derailed him; that had been her style since day one. Rhys turned away from the window. "How do you know this?"

"I saw her today at the station. They brought her in to give her statement. She looked...*strong*."

"She's always been strong," Rhys said, returning to his seat.

"And about moving to Sacramento," Archer said. "I'm not

sure if that's the wisest idea." At Rhys' arched eyebrow, Archer added, "After Hunt told me about Jake's arrest, I did a little digging. Zoey flew back to New York City this morning, but she also came with the two suitcases she left with."

Rhys couldn't move, couldn't breathe.

"All right, Rhys, I need to go to one of your meetings, so I need to run," William said, sidling up to the group.

"No."

William's brows went up. "No?"

"No to all of it," Rhys said and smiled at his inner circle of friends. "Looks like I'm staying in New York City after all."

A long pause. Then William reached into his pocket, concern heavy on his face. "That's it. You've fucking lost it. I'm calling your mother."

Kieran jumped up from his seat and wrapped an arm around William's neck. "Come on, Willie, tuck that phone away, and I'll grab ya another drink."

Rhys turned his attention to Hunt. "Where's Zoey now?"

"I suspect she's still at the station," Hunt replied.

Archer rose. "What do you need from us?"

Rhys glanced at his cousin. "Get William drunk enough that he passes out. He's going to talk to my parents, and I'd like to talk with Zoey before that happens."

Hunt cocked his head, well aware of what Rhys's family was like and how they'd react if William called them. "To prepare her for the Harrington storm coming her way?"

Rhys would need to explain why he'd been so wishy-washy to his parents. But there was one thing to take care of before he did that, and Zoey played a huge part in it. Rhys chuckled. "Yeah, something like that."

CHAPTER 15

"*T*hank you for your statement, Ms. Parker. You can leave now."

Zoey rose from her seat in the New York City Police Department, feeling like a weight had been lifted off her chest, but she didn't touch the USB stick that sat on the table between her and the detectives. The evidence of Rhys' conversation with Scott and Jake would no doubt get a conviction against Jake. She left the two stoic detectives behind in the cold room and headed down the hallway. All the fear, all the shame, no longer felt buried. Freedom made the world vivid again.

"Zoey, honey, we're over here."

She turned, seeing her parents in the waiting room. Warmth filled her as she hurried to their side, moving immediately into their arms. She never could have imagined her parents' supportive reaction. Or the outcome of revealing the truth. That, while she had exposed herself to the world, telling the truth made her feel safer. Made her feel free. She felt the power of each word she spoke during her statement.

Maybe it wasn't the revenge she'd once thought she deserved, but she knew she had taken a step to make the world a better place. To keep other women safe. Part of Jake's control had been to shame her so she buried her secret.

Not anymore. Never again.

"We're so proud of you, sweetie," said her mom, giving Zoey a big kiss on the cheek.

"Thanks." She stepped back, sighing heavily. "Honestly, I'm just glad that's all over. Those detectives are intense."

"You did good," her dad said, ushering them through another door. "I can only imagine how intimidating that interview must have been."

"Just a little," Zoey admitted with a soft laugh.

When they moved out to the large, open foyer of the police station, Hilary rose from the couch near the wall of windows. "Did it go okay?" she asked after rushing forward and gathering Zoey in her arms.

"Yeah," Zoey said, hugging her back. "It felt good to say what happened aloud. Actually, easier than I was expecting."

"I know exactly what you mean," Hilary said, backing away. "Feels good to stick it to him, right?"

Zoey laughed softly. "Definitely."

"Hey, Hil."

Hilary glanced over her shoulder, and Zoey caught sight of a cute guy waving at Hilary. "That's my boyfriend, Nathan," Hilary explained. "I'm sure with Jake's trial, we'll be seeing a lot of each other, but let's plan a dinner or something soon."

Hilary didn't know Zoey had ever left New York City, and Zoey didn't feel like explaining it all anyway. "I'd love that. I'll reach out soon."

"Please do. You killed it today. I'm so proud of you," said Hilary, giving Zoey another tight hug before she was off and running into her boyfriend's arms. Their laughter echoed in the large foyer. A different kind of warmth touched Zoey's chest now. It occurred to her that justice wasn't always about putting someone behind bars; it was about being heard. About being believed. An obvious weight had been lifted off Hilary too.

"Oh, there's the lawyer," her dad said. "I'll see what he needs." He dropped a kiss on Zoey's forehead and headed toward her lawyer with her mom in tow.

"You should have told me."

Zoey's eyes shut, a swell of emotion washing over her. She'd recognize that low voice anywhere.

"Zoey," he said again, so softly, a sound only for her.

She turned, meeting Rhys' warm stare. He wore black slacks and a gray button-up that did amazing things for his eyes. He held out a piece of paper. "What is this?" she asked.

He closed the distance. "My plane ticket to Sacramento. Like I said, you should have told me you were coming back."

She blinked, processed, and blinked again. "You were flying out to see me?"

"Not see you." He slid a hand low on her back, tugging her tightly against him. "I was going to Sacramento and never planning on coming back." He dropped his mouth, bringing his lips close to hers. "Imagine my surprise when I learned you decided to move back."

"How did you—" She laughed, knowing the answer. "Archer?"

"He does know all." Rhys grinned. His gaze followed his hand as he brushed her hair away from her face and tucked it behind her ear. Then his smile fell when he slid his knuckles across her cheek. "You're so brave to come forward, Zoey. That took such strength. I'm so proud of you."

Warmth touched all the cold bits she once felt deep in her chest. "I thought everything would fall apart once I told the truth, but it didn't." She took a step closer, wrapping her arms around him, not wanting to let go. "Telling the truth stitched me back together again. It brought me home."

"There is no better news than that." He dropped his head into her neck and held her tight.

For all that had felt wrong since she left New York City, everything felt instantly right again. She leaned her head against his chest, closed her eyes, and fell into him. "I wanted to tell you the plan, but I had to do this on my own."

"I know."

She leaned away, locking herself into the strength of his stare. "What if I told you I was done with fighting my way through life alone?"

"Then, I would tell you that you don't have to anymore." The sweetest smile she'd ever seen spread across his face before his lips met hers. She let him take her far, far away from there.

Until someone cleared their throat next to them.

Her dad said, "If you're kissing my daughter like that, I should at least meet you."

Zoey broke away, laughing. "Sorry, Dad. Rhys, I'd like you to meet my father, Daniel Parker, and my mother, Monica Parker."

Rhys shook both of their hands with all his bursting charm and incredible smile. "It's my pleasure to meet you."

Her mom gave Rhys a long examination. "So, you're the Rhys Harrington I've heard all about."

"Yes, indeed, I am," he said, his gaze turning contemplative before he faced her father. "If I've learned one thing from your daughter, it's that no matter what plans you have, they can always change. While I had other ideas about how this would go, I suppose having you here saves me a step." He sent Zoey a dazzling smile before addressing her father again. "Sir, I'd like your blessing to ask your daughter to marry me."

Her mom squealed, her hands covering her face.

Zoey blinked frantically, wondering if she'd heard him wrong.

The world spun away as Rhys continued, "You don't know me yet, but I promise to take care of Zoey. To treat her with the same love and respect you've obviously shown her. Most of all, I promise to give her the life she deserves." He hesitated, shooting her an intense look that stole her breath before adding to her father, "We don't need to rush this. I'm sure you want to get to know me, but if she agrees, I can't fathom spending another day not knowing that she'll be my wife."

"Oh, Daniel," her mother said, grabbing her father's arm.

Zoey still blinked, knowing she should say something, *do something*, but only managed to gawk.

Her father laughed at whatever crossed Zoey's face. "By the way she looks right now, I'd say you've done something right so far, son. But this choice is, and always will be, Zoey's."

Time slowed as Rhys moved in front of her and bent down on one knee in the foyer of the police station, not seeming to care that a crowd had gathered. "There are far more romantic ways of doing this, but you know, and I know, all that matters is the happiness we've found in each other. You left once. I'm damn determined to never let that happen again." He opened a box, revealing a princess-cut diamond ring. "Zoey, I have fallen wildly in love with you. Nothing makes sense without you. Everything is right when you're close. We deserve a win in life. Will you marry me?"

Zoey stared into Rhys' smoky eyes and said the easiest thing she'd ever said in her life, "Yes." Because when the bad had happened, the good seemed so far away. Now he was right there, offering her a lifetime of happiness, and she knew she'd fallen for him too. She threw her arms around him, hearing her mother crying beside her. "I love you, Rhys," she said in his ear.

He caught her in his arms and kissed the ticklish spot on her neck. "I love you, Zoey."

CHAPTER 16

*L*ater that night, sitting behind his desk in his office in Phoenix, Rhys was unsurprised when both his parents demanded to talk through Zoom. He wanted to give Zoey some time to process the engagement before she had to face his parents, but as was his life, his family wouldn't wait. While they were decent people, they were also spoiled, entitled, and most times, a lot to handle. For now, Zoey stood off to the side of his desk, biting her thumb, her worried eyes never leaving Rhys. He wasn't nearly as worried and found her concern endearing. She didn't want to disappoint, but how could she? She'd bewitched him from day one. Rhys had no doubt his parents would eventually fall under her spell too, once they got past the fact he was marrying a woman below his social status.

"We've got a lot to discuss, son," Warren Harrington said, sitting at a desk with an abstract art piece behind him. Rhys had always looked like his father. The gray eyes were a Harrington trait. Same body structure, same height, the only differences between them were his father had salt and pepper hair and a rounder jaw than Rhys'.

Sitting next to him, on a wing-back chair, Alice barely contained herself. "Sorry, did you just say you're *engaged?*" His mother's light-blue eyes were huge, her face barely moving from the Botox that kept her looking like she was in her forties.

"You heard me right," Rhys confirmed. He didn't need to explain anything to his family. He only owed explanations to his chosen family, but he wanted this to go smoothly for Zoey. Only for her, did he indulge this conversation at all. "Her name is Zoey Parker. She lives in Brooklyn. We've been seeing each other for the last month."

"A month." Alice gasped, glancing between Rhys and Warren. "Rhys, isn't that a bit quick?"

"Certainly is," he agreed.

"And you're sure about her?" Alice asked.

"Quite sure," was Rhys' reply.

Warren scrubbed at his smooth face, his eyes lifting to the ceiling. "Parker, hmm." His steely gaze returned to Rhys. "That's not a name I recognize. You said she's from Brooklyn. What does her family do?"

Rhys smiled. "You don't know the name because, I suspect, you've never met anyone like her."

"Rhys." His father frowned. "You know how we do things. We've got close connections in New York City to some predominant families."

At his father's ludicrous statement, Zoey shifted nervously on her feet and bowed her head. Yeah, that wasn't going to happen. Rhys had Zoey in his arms in a second flat. She fought him every step of the way until he had her in his lap, facing the monitor.

Both his parents looked mortified that she heard what they'd said. Rhys didn't plan on sugarcoating anything. To be with him, Zoey had to see what she was up against. Yes, he'd protect her from their entitlement, showing they were a solid front and Rhys was his own man, but she was in his life now. And his parents needed to get on board.

At the heavy silence, Zoey lifted her hand and waved. "Hi, I'm Zoey. It's great to meet you."

Silence.

Rhys chuckled and tucked her hair behind her ear. "Zoey is a dog groomer."

His mother made a noise.

His father arched a brow. "A dog groomer?"

"One of the best in Brooklyn," Rhys said.

Zoey laughed nervously, looking about ready to jump out of her skin. "Well, I *was* a dog groomer. I really loved it too. Great job. I met so many amazing people. But I actually applied for vet school this morning. I won't hear back for a month or so, but I was accepted once. Hopefully, I'll be accepted again."

Rhys placed a finger under her chin and turned her head, garnering her attention. "You applied to vet school?"

She gave him a smile that broke his world apart. "Well, you see, that money I got from that investment, instead of buying a house with it, I decided the absolute best way to spend it was to go to vet school."

"Zoey," Rhys said, bursting with pride he'd never felt before. "That's amazing."

She turned back to his parents, and the cute shyness faded a little as she added to Warren. "You asked before what my parents do for a living. They're both doctors in Sacramento."

Warren gave an unamused look to Rhys. "I suppose that explains why William thought you'd lost your mind. He sent me a blabbering text that you were moving to Sacramento. Nothing made any sense."

"We think he was drunk," Alice offered.

Rhys restrained his chuckle. He'd have to thank the guys

later. "I decided that staying in New York City suited me better."

"Good," Warren said in a hard voice. "We need Harrington blood in the city."

Rhys ignored that comment and looked at his mother as she asked Zoey in a sweeter voice than before, "What sort of doctors are your parents, Zoey?"

"My mom's a family doctor. She has her own practice, and my dad's a vascular surgeon."

"How interesting," Alice said with a tender smile. "I suppose we'll have to arrange to meet them."

Zoey returned the smile. "I'm sure they would love to meet you both."

Alice glanced at Rhys then at Warren then at Zoey. "Well, there is much to do to plan a wedding."

"No," Rhys said.

Warren's brows shot up. "No?"

"No planning," Rhys said, kissing Zoey's shoulder. He fought his grin at the way she wiggled against him. He looked at his father. "No big production. We're having a private ceremony with close friends only. Both of you are welcome to attend." He appreciated what his parents had given to him growing up. He'd always do what needed to be done to keep the Harrington name a solid force in New York City. But his life was his own, and Zoey was all that mattered now.

His father grimaced.

Alice couldn't sit still. She eventually broke the heavy silence and asked, "That's what you want, then, Rhys?"

"That's what *we* want."

He smiled at Zoey as she wrapped her arms around him. She looked at his mother and asked, "Will you be back in the city anytime soon? I have no doubt my mom will fly in for dress shopping. We'd love for you to join us."

Alice blinked, exchanged a long look with Warren, and blinked again at Zoey. "I can try my best to make that happen."

"Excellent," Rhys said. To his father, he added, "Anything else to discuss?"

Warren shook his head. "I believe all our bases are covered." He hesitated a beat. Then did the most unexpected thing. He smiled. "Congratulations on your engagement. Would you allow me to announce it in the newspaper?"

Rhys had to process the fact that his father had asked him a question, instead of demanding something. He smiled back. "Yes, that would be fine."

"Then, it'll be done."

They said quick goodbyes with his mother still seeming shell-shocked that Zoey wanted to involve her in something so personal. Rhys put his computer to sleep and sat back in his chair, shifting Zoey on his lap until she was straddling him. Her eyes held him captive. "You didn't have to tell them your parents are doctors. You don't have to feed into their entitled behavior."

She kissed his nose. "Yes, I did. That's the type of people they are. It didn't hurt me to reassure them."

He stared at her, absolutely bewildered by her strong character. This amazing woman who'd blindsided him wholeheartedly, giving him this life, this love, he never believed he'd find.

She laughed softly, tapping the side of his face. "What's that look for?"

"This whole time, you kept saying I was helping you, but in reality, it seems like you're fixing all the cracks in my life."

"Good," she said, lacing her fingers behind his neck. "It levels the playing field."

He chuckled, tempted to stay right there, only he had a

plan for tonight. One that had his cock twitching in eagerness. "Speaking of playing, we are due downstairs."

She tilted her head. "We are?"

"Mm-hmm." He straightened in the seat until he cupped her face and brought her mouth close to his. "Tonight, Phoenix will learn that you are mine and I am yours. But the choice will always be yours." He arched an eyebrow. "What do you say, Zoey? Yes or no to my game tonight?"

"Yes," she said, brushing her lips against his. "Always yes, Rhys."

CHAPTER 17

*S*ensual music played through the speakers as Zoey entered the private room at Phoenix. She was wearing black lingerie paired with a black metal butterfly masquerade mask and stilettos, only this time, the members weren't hidden; they were all there, standing in typical Phoenix attire of lingerie for the women and black slacks for the men, waiting...*watching*. Candles lit a path forward to a circular table. On that table was a glass of wine. Beyond that was a view Zoey had a hard time believing was real. Rhys sat on a chair, naked, his arms bound behind him, a black gag covering his mouth, and a Venetian mask on his face. And something she'd told him once filled her mind: *"I like watching her control him like that."* More importantly, she recalled his reply: *"Would you like to own me like that, Zoey. To control me? To do whatever you want to me?"* As she slowly approached the table in the center of the room, it occurred to her that Rhys was giving her exactly what she'd asked for.

When she stopped in front of the single wineglass, the world slowed. To all those in the room, except for Rhys' inner circle of friends, the significance of the wine would be unknown. No one knew what Zoey did. That Rhys had asked for one thing going forward: her trust. She looked at the wineglass, waiting for her heart to race, for the desire to run to rush over her. It never came. She took hold of the glass and looked into Rhys' fierce stare as she took a long sip before lowering the drink back to the table. His emotion-packed eyes pulled her forward, but with every step she took, she felt more free, like she was shedding the parts of herself that Jake and Scott had hurt. Now she was stepping into the future. With Rhys.

The sensual energy in the room washed over her, taking her to a place where she left all her inhibitions, all her insecurities at the door. She felt every muscle in her body working to get to Rhys. Every single beat of her heart. She focused on the breath sliding through her lungs. The magic that this crowd created, the freedom she felt. When she stopped in front of him, she stared into his smoky gray eyes that promised her the world. And she wanted to give him the world back.

Now in front of him, she understood the meaning of the silk gag in his mouth. That tonight she had full control, but she realized she didn't want that. "I always want to hear your voice," she said, untying the silk from behind his head and letting it fall to the ground.

"You drank the wine," he said, no question in his voice, only pride.

"I drank what you gave to me."

Something rich and real passed in the air between them. Something Zoey now knew was love. True love. Impossible love. Love that came from two broken souls that found all the pieces they needed to heal. She didn't question her love for Rhys, and she didn't want to draw this out. The show might be for others, but ultimately, she knew this show belonged to them. Always to them.

She slid onto his lap, reaching for the condom on the tray next to them. A condom was Phoenix protocol. She slid it into place onto his hard cock and didn't bother teasing him. She rose up on her toes and took Rhys deep inside her, their moans echoing around them.

She dropped her head back, sensing all the eyes on her. And this time, she felt powerful, not the shy woman who'd once walked through Phoenix's doors looking for justice. As she rose up and slowly lowered down onto him, his rough growl washed over her. Within that sound, she truly understood what Phoenix offered. Why so many people protected this place. In a world full of judgment and negativity, this space had none of it. There was only the beauty of sensual beings who enjoyed flesh and lust and everything in between.

Rhys' continued groans caused goosebumps to appear across her skin as she tested how to ride him. Up and down, circling over her hips, shifting back and forth. She'd seen videos, but this was all for her own exploration. And soon, the slowness of their embrace became not enough. She saw the flex of Rhys' muscles, the quiver of his body as he fought against the binds holding him. She lifted her hands to Rhys' neck, noting the bulging veins beneath her touch. Holding his gaze, captivated by the love staring back at her, she began to bounce. The fullness of Rhys became exactly what she needed. What she craved. And she moved faster now, harder.

Under his powerful stare, she found everything she'd ever wanted and all the things she didn't know she needed. He was her protector, her savior, and she knew for certain, she was his *home.* The one he'd almost had, but was stolen away. The one he deserved as a child. The one she would make safe and warm for him.

Lost in all her emotions and the truth of what they gave to each other, she dropped her mouth to his. Through every rock of her hips, she let go of all her insecurities, her hesitations, her worries. To the one man who deserved her without restraint, she gave the eroticism she knew he hungered. "Come for me, Rhys," she said roughly in his ear.

She lifted up, leaning back to ride him hard, fast, massaging her breasts with her hands. His gaze flicked to her chest, his pupils enlarged and darkened with lust as his muscles flexed once more against the bindings holding him. His teeth bit down on his bottom lip, his masculine grunts a sound Zoey would chase forever.

Leaning forward, she gave his neck a hard nip and demanded in his ear, "Don't make me wait."

Not a second after, his body tensed, trembled, and then he roared, every muscle in his spectacular body stretching over taut skin. And she went over the edge with him.

Sometime later, voices and moans drifted into Zoey's ears as Rhys chuckled against her neck. "Look behind you."

Breathless, Zoey found the strength to glance back and couldn't stop her surprised gasp. Behind them, an orgy had erupted. Some couples were already having sex. One woman was giving a man a blow job while another man had his head buried between her thighs. She knew Hunt, Kieran, Archer, and Lottie were in there somewhere, but she couldn't make anyone out. All she saw was skin, passion, and pleasure.

Rhys chuckled again, drawing her gaze back to him. "It seems every rule gets broken when you're around."

She laughed softly, her legs feeling like jelly, but she didn't want to move, not yet. "Well, the rule really is that no one can touch the participants in the show. Besides, you can't really blame them. Look at you. Anyone watching you would be driven wild."

"Me?" He retorted with a dry laugh. "Zoey, that was all you. The beauty of you. The sensuality of you. The inno-cence. It's captivating, not only to me."

"No, Rhys, that was all you. The strength of you. The eroticism of you. The power. It's captivating, not only to me."

He tossed his head back and chuckled freely. "Then, shall we say it's *us* that drive people wild?"

"Yes," she agreed with every mended part of her heart. "It'll always be us. Forever, Rhys."

"Forever, Zoey."

EPILOGUE

"That's the last of it," Rhys said, dropping the final box onto his kitchen floor a few days later. "Feels like home yet?" he asked, pulling Zoey in close.

"You're here, so yes." Happiness spread across her like a warm bath as she leaned up and pulled his face down for a kiss. Everything was perfect. Sure, moving out of the loft came with a little sadness, but at least, she was only a subway ride away, instead of states away. Besides, the truth was they were all so happy Zoey came back it didn't matter where she lived. And Zoey was absolutely certain about marrying Rhys and sharing her life with him. She was even happy to be living in Manhattan, something she never thought she'd be able to feel here.

"You two are so stinkin' cute," said Hazel, opening up one of the boxes to help Zoey settle in. Hunt was helping her. "Your entire love story is just so wild and perfect and just all the wonderful things."

"Thanks, Hazel," Zoey said, releasing Rhys to give her a tight squeeze. "But you're still going to come over for cuddles, right?"

"Yes, to cuddles." Hazel gave a knowing look and pointed at the pool outside. "But I also see poolside margaritas in our future."

"Oh, I'm so here for that," Elise said from the kitchen, where she began unwrapping Zoey's favorite mug.

"Yes—"

The front door slamming open cut Zoey off. Archer stormed in, ready to kill someone. The vein in the middle of his forehead looked like it pulsed. "Where is she?" he growled.

Rhys' brows shot up. "Where is who?"

"I suspect he's looking for me," Elise said, raising her hand.

Archer took a few steps farther into the condominium and slammed the door shut behind him. His knuckles were white, his body trembling slightly. His eyes narrowed into slits at Elise. "You…"

Elise grinned, batting her lashes at him. "Hello, Archer."

Thick silence filtered into the room. No one dared break it. Not with Archer looking a second away from smashing something or punching a wall. His nostrils flared. "You think you're funny?"

"Most days, I'm utterly hilarious," Elise said, leaning her hip against the countertop, still grinning. All teeth.

Zoey glanced between them, barely able to breathe against the tension in the room. "Do you know what happened?" she asked Rhys.

He shrugged, eyes set firmly on Archer.

"What happened?" Archer snapped, his eyes bulging out. "What happened is that woman," he pointed at Elise like he held a dagger in his hand, "signed me up for every woman's magazine subscription on the fucking planet. I have spent the last three hours trying to get out of the yearly subscriptions."

Silence descended until Hunt roared with laughter, and everyone followed suit.

Elise grinned from ear to ear, her eyes dancing. "Sucks, right? Having someone invade your life and make choices for you."

"Nothing about this is funny, Elise," Archer growled. "I didn't do anything like this to you."

Elise hesitated, scrunching her nose, then shrugged. "Well, it *is* kind of funny, and yes, you did do the exact same thing. Do I need to remind you that you got your dirty hackers to hack into my personal computer?"

"My hackers aren't dirty."

Elise gave him a bored look, reaching for another news-paper-covered mug in the box. "They are as dirty as they come. They do bad shit. And they were inside my personal computer!" She looked back up at Archer, her gaze flipping him off. "You don't like me going into your personal life, stay out of mine."

Zoey watched the stare down. She turned to Rhys next to her. "They're going to kill each other."

"It's likely." He watched them a moment more and shook his head, laughing. "Or fuck the living shit out of each other. One of the two."

Kieran walked through the door, carrying pizzas on top of a big box, a deep frown marring his face. "Yeah, thanks for the help there, Archer."

Archer still glared at Elise.

Always wanting everyone to be happy, Hazel laughed awkwardly. She rushed to Kieran's side and took the pizza boxes. "Thanks for picking up the pizza," she said to him.

"Not a problem." He winked at her.

She blushed.

Kieran grinned at her retreating form. Was Hazel wiggling her hips a little more than necessary?

Zoey basked in all the happiness. For a long time, it had only been her, Elise, and Hazel. Now their days included these men, and she couldn't wait to see what would happen for them next. Things really did have a funny way of working themselves out. She slid her arms around Rhys' middle and said quietly to him, "Archer and Elise are ready to kill each other. Kieran's making Hazel blush. And Hunt's about to eat that entire pizza to himself. I guess this is our life now, huh?"

Rhys chuckled, wrapped his arm around Zoey, bringing her close, and dropped a kiss on her forehead. "Yeah, and I wouldn't change it for anything in the world."

She glanced out at Hazel, who was still blushing, and Elise ignoring Archer like he wasn't burning a hole in the back of her head, and she smiled. "Yeah, me neither."

Thank you for reading!

CLICK HERE TO SUBSCRIBE TO MY MAILING LIST TO NEVER MISS A NEW RELEASE & YOU'LL GET A FREE READ TOO!

ABOUT THE AUTHOR

Stacey Kennedy is a *USA Today* bestselling author who writes contemporary romances full of heat, heart, and happily ever afters. With over 50 titles published, her books have hit Amazon, B&N, and Apple Books bestseller lists.

Stacey lives with her husband and two children in south-western Ontario—in a city that's just as charming as any of the small towns she creates. Most days, you'll find her enjoying the outdoors with her family or venturing into the forest with her horse, Priya. Stacey's just as happy curled up indoors, where she writes surrounded by her lazy dogs. She believes that sexy books about hot cowboys or alpha heroes can fix any bad day. But wine and chocolate help too.

ACKNOWLEDGMENTS

To my husband, my children, family, friends, and bestie, it's easy to write about love when there is so much love around me. Big thanks to my readers for your friendship and your support; my editor, Lexi, for making my stories shine; my agent, Jessica, for always having my back; my cover artist, Regina, who never ceases to amaze me with her beautiful work; my PR company, Social Butterfly, I'd be lost without you; the kick-ass authors in my sprint group for their endless advice and support; and to Christa, who helped me brainstorm the idea for this series. Thank you.

READ THE NEXT BOOK IN STACEY
KENNEDY'S PHOENIX SERIES:

KEEP ME

CHAPTER 1

"I'll take an Old Forester on the rocks," Archer said to the bartender of the classy New York City cigar lounge.

Fitz, a long-time employee of the cigar lounge, smiled. "Coming right up." He looked plucked from a different era with his handlebar mustache curling up at the ends and his wise, amber-colored eyes.

The cigar lounge was full of customers tonight, sitting at the round tables, enjoying fine alcohol, ice clinking against their glasses. Smoke billowed from the table next to Archer as the customer lit his cigar, infusing the air with an aroma of burnt coffee and a hint of cinnamon. Soft jazz played from the speakers set high on the walls around the room. Three bartenders dressed in tuxes served up drinks while waiters tended to the customers at the tables. Back when the cigar lounge had been constructed in the 1920s, this spot was a gentleman's club. Now the lounge was a local hotspot. But what was truly special about this building was beneath the shiny hardwood floors. Phoenix, the ultra-exclusive, upscale sex club, only accessible through tunnels once used to bootleg whiskey into the club. Each member was able to request one sex show per month—sex acts, participants, every little detail was of the member's preference, something both Archer and Fitz were long-time participants in. All the members were put through a government-level vetting process before they gained access to Phoenix.

As Fitz fetched Archer's drink, the cigar lounge's door opened and Archer was immediately drawn to the woman in the tight jeans, high heels, and black blouse that showed an enticing hint of cleavage. He had fought in elite missions during his time in the United States Army Special Forces. He knew how to plan a dangerous mission and execute it with flawless precision. But the woman before him, with her long dark-brown hair—that just reached her heart-shaped ass— and sharp dark chocolate-colored brown eyes made his head spin. Elise Fanning, the sexiest, most irritating woman he'd ever met in his twenty-nine years.

When he'd first learned her name from Wayne after she hacked into Phoenix's security, he took the breach person- ally. Until he found out the reason why she'd broken through his firewall. Elise's best friend, Zoey Parker, had needed to gain membership to confront two members who had wronged her. If it had been Archer's choice, Zoey would have been banned from Phoenix immediately. As it was, Rhys Harrington, Phoenix's owner, felt a connection to Zoey. A connection that had led to their engagement last week.

In the weeks that followed the hacking, security had been stepped up to ensure no one slid past Phoenix's defenses again. But since the security breach, Zoey had seamlessly blended her friends with Rhys', and that meant Archer had gotten to know Elise on a personal level. First, she had gotten under his skin with her sass and snark and her ability to outsmart him at every turn, including finding a way past his security. Then she got into his head by being the most curious creature he'd ever met. He wanted to peel back all her layers until he had her naked, exposed—emotionally and physically—and begging for his mouth all over her lush body.

"Anything else for tonight?"

He snapped his eyes back to Fitz and shook his head. "No, thank you."

Fitz's mouth curved at the corner, his gaze flicking to Elise. "A sweet little thing catch your eye?"

"Ha! Sweet?" Archer took a long sip of the bourbon in his glass, catching the spicy notes in the dark amber-colored liquor. "That woman is many things, but sweet is not among them." Cutthroat, wicked smart, and in possession of bigger balls than some men Archer knew.

Fitz chuckled.

Archer's eyes stayed locked on an approaching Elise. Two months ago, Archer would never have believed they were a good match. She couldn't stand him, and he couldn't stand that she'd somehow broken through security he thought unbreakable. But damn, she was fiery and smart and sexy, and his cock hardened in mere seconds of being around her. A reaction she apparently shared as a slight color rose to her cheeks under his watchful stare. "Good evening, Elise," he said when she reached him.

She met him with dark eyes that had the power to freeze him where he stood. "Hello, Archer."

A shudder ran through him at his name on her tongue. Being the center of this woman's attention meant something, demanded a man take notice. "Thank you for coming to see me tonight," he said.

"No problem," she said, sliding onto the stool next to him, facing him. "I'll take a Jim Beam, neat," she said to Fitz. Soft voices drifted over from the table behind them while she watched him with those soul-penetrating eyes that leveled his defenses. Once Fitz delivered her drink and headed off to serve another customer, she added, "I've got to admit, I was surprised that you called me."

"I've got a problem," he told her.

Elise flashed a wicked grin. "A subscription to a women's magazine problem?"

He restrained himself from rolling his eyes. A few days ago, Wayne had delivered a final report on Elise, including details he got off her personal computer. When she discovered her computer had been hacked and Archer was the one behind it, she reciprocated by signing him up for dozens of women's magazine subscriptions. Getting out of those subscriptions had been nothing less than a giant pain in his ass. Four of them were still outstanding, and Archer, for his pride alone, had given in to paying them instead of fighting his way out of the subscriptions. And yet...*and yet*, while they might have come to a truce, and even if it irritated him, she'd impressed him. Not that he'd tell her that. "No, in fact, that problem has been handled," he replied dryly.

She laughed easily, like she didn't have a care in the world. Her long, spectacular legs crossed. "All right, I give. What's the problem?"

"I've got a person I'd like investigated. I need your help."

Her amused expression faltered a moment, surprise glinting in her powerful eyes. "Let me make sure I've got this right. You need *my* help?"

He didn't want to admit it, certainly not to her, but his investigation into her had left only one conclusion: Elise was the best private investigator in the state. Not only did he want to ally himself with her to further protect Phoenix and use her skills to do so, but hiring her gave him a means to get closer to her. "I do, and it requires confidentiality."

Intrigue sparkled in her eyes. "I'm listening. Go on."

"The details are..."—he gestured to all the people around them—"sensitive. Let's take this to my office."

She polished off her drink, then rose. "Lead the way."

He downed the rest of his bourbon and then made his way to the door on the far side, and after he entered in the security code, she followed him inside. The noise from the lounge quieted as he entered his office, which used to be one of the private rooms in the gentleman's club. Old leather-bound books lined the walls surrounding the grand cherry-wood desk set near the thin, tall window. Archer skipped his desk and headed for the sitting area with the two brown wingback chairs. He waited for Elise to sit before he joined her and got right to the point. "I've grown suspicious about a member of the club."

"Why? What's happened?" she asked.

"The other night, this person brought her own mask into the club instead of using the ones provided." Every Phoenix member wore a mask. Some, who required their identity hidden, wore full ones. Some demonic and some animalistic. The rest wore simple masquerade masks, being a little more revealing of their identities. "The incident went unnoticed for an hour before one of my security guards picked up on it and we brought her in for questioning."

Elise sat back against her chair, studying him, her expression a well-crafted poker face. "Uh-oh, someone get fired?"

"Suspended for two weeks," he said. His team was composed of retired military who took their failures seriously. Mistakes happened, but they only happened once under Archer's authority. And nothing from the outside was ever allowed inside. Phoenix provided expensive lingerie, masks, anything a member could want. The only exemption were the men's dark slacks, and those were searched methodically for bugs, recording devices, anything that could comprise security. "She brought the mask in a purse that wasn't searched, and that is inexcusable."

Elise watched him for a long moment. "Tell me why this mask worries you."

He rose and moved to his desk, taking out the gold-and-black object in the plastic bag from his locked filing cabinet. "Her behavior was off during questioning," he said, returning to Elise and offering her the mask.

"Off, how?"

"Nervous, edgy." He returned to his seat. "We scanned it for bugs, a camera, anything electronic. We found nothing. I've dug as far as I can go into this member's life, and nothing is showing up that would raise alarms. She said she didn't know the rules about not being able to bring in her own mask, and right now, there's nothing to suggest that's not the truth."

"But your instincts tell you otherwise?"

He nodded, not surprised she'd caught on. Elise's quick mind was what made her stand out. "Everything about this member has me on edge. Something's not right here. I can feel it." He leaned forward, resting his elbows on his knees, leveling her with a measured look. "So, Rhys asked me to extend you an offer. That you investigate this member and that if this job goes well, the club would use your services exclusively going forward." Only because Archer had suggested it to Rhys. Archer was only as good as his team, and Elise had proven herself invaluable.

No wise businessperson would turn down the offer he presented. Phoenix was home to multi-millionaires who paid a pretty penny to stay out of the media. Anyone working in security for the club made a six-figure income, including Archer.

Elise studied him and then the mask. "Can I take this to examine it?"

He nodded. "Of course."

She placed it in her purse before a deep breath spilled

from her pouty lips. "All right, I'll look into this for you. But I need you to do two things for me."

He doubted he was going to like either of the things she wanted. "Name them."

"Get me into the club," she said without a flicker of emotion on her face.

"As a member?" he asked to clarify.

She gave him a flat look. "No, not as a member. I have no interest in watching other people fuck."

Don't knock it until you try it. "For investigatory reasons, then?"

"Exactly," she said with a nod. "Don't tell me the name of this woman or anything about her."

"You don't want to know the name of the woman you're investigating?"

She shook her head. "Let me study the members in person to see if anyone stands out on odd behavior alone." She paused to shrug. "I'm a people reader, and I'm good at it."

He didn't doubt her. She seemed to read straight through him all too easily and knew exactly how to irritate him as much as possible. She was always, in everything she did, one step ahead of him. At first, he'd hated that. He still hated that, but a new sensation burned alongside his annoyance—*desire*. Even now, behind those clever sparkling eyes, he knew she had a plan, a way to manipulate the whole world to her advantage. All he wanted was a single peek into her brilliant mind. "All right, done. And the second request?"

A slow smile filled her face. A hissing kitten would have looked friendlier. "Tell me."

He frowned. "Tell you what?"

"Tell me why you're asking *me* of all people to do this."

Poking his tongue lightly into his cheek, he inhaled deeply. This woman would be the death of him. "Seriously, Elise, you're going to make me say it?"

She gave a firm nod and a wicked grin. "Oh, hell yes, I'm going to make you say it."

"Unbelievable," he muttered, watching her closely. While he did need her help, he needed to level the playing field, so he rose and settled himself in front of her chair. Placing his hands on both armrests, he leaned down. She straightened at his nearness, and her breath hitched when he brought his face down to hers and said, "Elise, you're the best PI out there, and I am desperately in need of your help." He arched an eyebrow, feeling her rapid warm breaths brushing across his face, certain that was lust burning in the depths of her eyes. "Will that suffice?"

Not one to shy away from a game, she rose and slid up against him sensually. "Yes, Archer, that will do. Text me the details when you know what night I'll be coming to the club."

Hard and annoyed that she had the power to even control his damn cock, Archer didn't dare step back. Neither did Elise. "You'll start on this right away?" he asked.

"I've got a current case to wrap up tomorrow morning, but I can begin in the afternoon."

Heat burned in the space between them, drawing him in. "Excellent."

Her gaze swept over his lips before lifting to his eyes again. "We'll talk soon, then."

"We will."

And like the vixen she was, her hand brushed against the front of his pants as she walked away. No doubt she'd felt every inch of his erection. An erection that didn't seem to understand this woman was a complete pain in his ass.

Printed in Great Britain
by Amazon